M. Steven S.

ILL
BEHAVIOR

CONTENTS

For Chelsea

Don't everybody like the smell of gasoline?
Well burn motherfucker burn American Dream

-André 3000, *Gasoline Dreams*

There's colors on the street
Red, white and blue
People shuffling their feet
People sleeping in their shoes

-Neil Young, *Rockin' in the Free World*

SELECTED LAWS

SELECTED SECTIONS OF HIS MAJESTY'S MUNICIPAL, ADMINISTRATIVE AND PENAL
CODES FOR THE CITY OF LOS ANGELES AND THE UNITED STATES CONSTITUTION

MUNI CODE, ARTICLE 14, SECTION 49.84.1

(A) His Majesty and the City Council of the City of Los Angeles
find graffiti on public or private property a blighting element that leads to
depreciation of the value of the defaced property and of the adjacent and
surrounding properties to the extent that graffiti creates a negative impact
on the entire city.

(B) His Majesty and the City Council find and determine that the
power of graffiti to create fear and insecurity within the community detracts
from the sense of community enjoyed by residents, making graffiti both a
property crime and a social crime impacting the quality of life and freedom
from intimidation that citizens desire and have a right to enjoy within their
neighborhoods.

ADMIN CODE, DIVISION 5, CHAPTER 152, SECTION 5.554

(b) There is hereby established an Oversight Committee comprised of
the Mayor of Los Angeles, the City Barrister, the Chief of Police, a Magistrate
Inquirer appointed by the City Council, and the Director of the Office of
Community Beautification, or their respective designated representatives,
to recommend actions and expenditures, to identify, organize, implement
and coordinate technology for the early identification, intervention and
apprehension of graffiti vandals.

ADMIN CODE, DIVISION 19, CHAPTER 12, SECTION 19.129.2

2. The City of Los Angeles may pay a reward of $2,500 for information
resulting in the identification, apprehension and conviction, or a final
adjudication by the Court, of, or as to, any person or persons whose acts of
graffiti-related vandalism or defacement as it pertains to the graffiti, have
damaged or destroyed public or private property in the City of Los Angeles.
The reward may be increased in the discretion of the City Council and in
consultation with the Oversight Committee.

(b)(3) if any person is convicted of the crime of vandalism in which the amount of damage is one million dollars ($1,000,000) or more, in the aggregate, or at such time when multiple convictions of such person equal or exceed such amount, then such person may be punished by a fine not to exceed two hundred fifty thousand dollars ($250,000), or by imprisonment not to exceed five years in jail. If such person fails to pay the total assessed fine within one year from the date of such assessment, or fails to timely report to the designated jail, then at the recommendation of the City Council, in consultation with the Oversight Committee, a panel of not less than three elected judges, by unanimous decision, may order the removal of such person's lesser-dominant hand.

Second Addendum to the First Amendment of The United States Constitution

Speech of a seditious nature carried out during the commission of a felony, or intended to incite imminent rebellion against His Majesty, is punishable by death by decapitation.

Chimes.

A soft jingle rings out at the opening of the door. A young man and a woman stumble into the shop in a stupor of spirits and flirtatious banter. The man peeks about the curious room as their lips mingle and tongues cavort.

Various forms of stars, triangles and crescent moons, and other odd shapes and symbols, dangle from the ceiling. Antique prints encased in simple, black frames hang on the walls. One of them contains a sketch of a human hand with lines diagrammed on the palm. At the top of the print is the phrase "Your fate awaits you." At the bottom is the word PALMISTRY. Another print contains the outline of the profile of a human head with androgynous facial features. The skull is divided into blobby, color-coded regions, each of which is further divided into splotchy districts. Each region and each district is labeled—words like Moral and Reflectives, and Animal and Perceptives. At the top of the print is the phrase "What lies within?" At the bottom, PHRENOLOGY.

The room is scarcely furnished. A settee of chestnut and white linen rests in an alcove under the storefront window. A maple credenza hosts a number of colorful stones and crystals. The tattered spines of old books are lined along a shelf. A table for two sits in the back corner of the room, draped with white lace. At the center of the table, a gleaming crystal ball balances on a plain wooden pedestal. The minimalist decor and tidy interior are out of step with the typical parlor of this sort.

The woman senses that the man is distracted. She pulls away from him, swinging frayed, dirty-blonde dreadlocks over one shoulder.

"What's wrong?"

"Nothing," he replies. "It's just … when you told me your shop was around the corner, I thought it was a bakery or a boutique. But … you're a fortune teller?"

"Something like that," she says, flipping her head toward the front window. The man reads the backward letters written in an arc over the image of an all-seeing eye, illuminated by a glowing streetlight: Oracle Dehlia.

"An oracle?" he scoffs. "In other words, you scam people for money."

"Not at all," Dehlia says, in a heard-it-all-before tone. She pulls the man close to her. "I assist them on their spiritual journey."

She kisses his neck then playfully shoves him down on the settee.

"Oh, really? And just how does one go about becoming an oracle?"

"Well, I wouldn't say I decided to become one. It just … happened."

"Uh-huh," he says with sardonic inflection.

"Seriously," she replies as she maneuvers onto his lap and straddles him face-to-face.

The man gently kneads her thighs as she continues her story.

"I was raised by my grandfather. I never knew my grandmother, but he used to tell me that she was related to the old oracles. My grandmother's grandmother told stories that were passed down from her grandmother, and her grandmother's grandmother, and … well, you get the gist. I always assumed they were just made-up tales that papu liked to tell me to let my imagination run wild, until …" She pauses in a state of reminiscence.

The man glimpses the slightest quiver in Dehlia's full lips.

"Until …" he gently probes.

Dehlia regains her train of thought, "Until I had a clairvoyant experience."

The man laughs. "Oh, c'mon, you don't really expect me to—"

"It's true," she interjects. "I was meditating with my boyfriend at the time. There we sat with our legs crossed and eyes closed. I was in aakaash mudra. It was a bright and breezy day and the sun felt good on my shoulders. About twenty minutes in, and I was in it deep, he reached out and touched my thigh. And at that very instant, I saw him die."

The man's skin erupts into goosebumps and he quickly lifts his hands from her thighs.

Dehlia half-smiles and presses his hands back down.

"I couldn't articulate it at the time. It was just a rush of feelings and fragmented images. But I very distinctly saw the light fade from his eyes, his face speckled with blood and his head lying on a dirty curb. I started crying and I tried to tell him what I saw and how it felt. He held me and tried to calm me down. He told me he believed that I felt something real, but he wrote it off as a bad daydream— that I probably fell asleep and was startled awake at the same instant some negative energy washed through me. But two months later, while he was walking home from a night out with his friends, a drunken teenager veered off the road and hit him."

"Oh my god."

"He died within minutes."

"I'm so sorry."

"It's okay. It seems like a lifetime ago. It's good to remember it now. To remember the night when I realized that what I had experienced was a premonition. The night I realized I may have a gift. Even though it's marked by tragedy."

The man nods his head, his face full of sympathy.

"So," she perks up, "ever since that night, I've been dedicated to exploring myself—to exploring what's within me … and within others. And here's where I'm likely going to lose you. I believe something's happening, Tyler. Something's awakening in our blood. Maybe not in everyone, but in some of us."

Tyler draws a breath and shakes his head. But before he's able to proffer a cynical quip, Dehlia cuts him off.

"Just hear me out. I noticed it in me, and so I started to seek out others like me—others who are introspective, who make it a point to search within themselves—and some of them, they've also noticed certain … occurrences."

"Where do you even begin to look for people like that?"

"Oh, certain bookstores and conventions … you know the type." Dehlia gestures toward the crystals sitting on the credenza behind her. "I know, I know, you don't believe in that sort of thing. Typical, just like how you Americans say you worship the old gods, but few of you actually believe in them. All I can tell you is that the gift is real—or is becoming real—and I've been able to develop it, little by little. It's not always reliable and it's still very much a mystery, but I can feel it growing. Sometimes it's as if my blood is whispering to me. That's why I opened up this shop—to help others, but also to help myself."

"How can any of this possibly be true? Surely if these gifts … or occurrences, or whatever … actually exist, many people would have had similar experiences and all of this would be common knowledge by now."

"That's a fair point," Dehlia replies. "And I don't know how it's possible. I wish I did, but"—Dehlia pauses to gather her thoughts— "I like to compare it to the udumbara tree."

Tyler shrugs and shakes his head.

"You see, in Buddhist mythology, the figs of the udumbara are said to contain a flower within them, hidden deep inside the fruit. It's said that the flower blossoms only once every three thousand years. So, the beauty of this otherwise normal-looking tree lies dormant for millennia, literally. Generations go by and the flower is all but forgotten, but that doesn't change the fact that the flower is real.

"Now, what if these gifts—these abilities of legend and myth— are also real? What if over time they simply went into a sort of hibernation and we forgot about them? What if they're buried somewhere deep in our DNA, or in the labyrinth of our grey matter, waiting to blossom again?"

Tyler nods in contemplation. "Just think of all the unseen flowers around us every day."

"Yes, exactly," Dehlia says, an aroused sparkle in her eyes. "So how about it?" She takes Tyler's hand and tenderly pries open his fingers and arches her brow. "Shall we see what's within you?"

"Oh, I don't—"

"Come now. Back at the bar, you told me you were here on a spiritual pilgrimage. Part of you wants to believe. And you can't leave Greece without having a self-proclaimed oracle read your palm, can you?"

Tyler searches her bright green eyes—eyes that have convinced so many of so much with that guileful gaze.

He surrenders.

"Yeah, okay … let's do it."

"Ade!"

Dehlia slides off of Tyler and onto the cushion next to him. Tyler begins to stand, but Dehlia grabs his hand and pulls him back.

"Where are you going?"

"To the table," Tyler says, pointing toward the crystal ball.

Dehlia smirks in amusement. "No, no. That's just for show—for those who need the ambiance to get into the moment. Here, sit and turn to me. Now, I need something from you. Something you carry with you often. A watch or a ring, something like that."

Tyler flips his hands over and says, "No watch, no jewelry— sorry, I didn't come prepared."

"Surely there's something we can use."

Tyler pats at his pockets and pulls out a thin wallet and his passport. The front of the passport reads: KINGDOM OF THE UNITED STATES OF AMERICA.

"Not what I had in mind, but it will have to do," Dehlia laments. She flips open the passport and looks at his picture. "Mmm, you're photogenic." She crinkles her face with surprise. "And young … barely twenty-four. Ba! I could practically be your mother."

Tyler grins, bashfully so.

"Close your eyes and make your mind still."

"Still?"

"Yes—calm, or empty." Dehlia strokes his palm with her index finger. "You're a painter," she says.

Tyler opens his eyes, looks at his hands, a bit of paint crusted around a couple of his fingernails. "Yes—because there's paint on my hands."

Dehlia blushes. "Sorry, just a habit. Keep your eyes closed."

She sets her hand on top of Tyler's open palm, her other hand holds his wallet and passport. She closes her eyes and the two of them sit in silence.

After a while, Dehlia says, flatly, "You've experienced a loss."

Yeah, but who hasn't, Tyler thinks to himself.

Dehlia's body begins to sway gently.

"You have a gift ... speech ... or communication. It's in you, but it has yet to bloom."

Tyler lifts his eyebrows at the assertion. Dehlia's gentle swaying evolves into a back-and-forth rocking.

"Something will go wrong for you. It will be as an omen and it will begin the end. And then they will come for you."

Tyler scrunches his face. Dehlia's rocking body becomes exaggerated and erratic, no clear rhythm to her movement.

"In a sea of drums and trumpets, you are a clashing cymbal."

Tyler cocks his head in response to the cryptic statement. He peeps open his eyelids and spies Dehlia—her eyes flitting vigorously behind closed eyelids. Her rocking becomes almost violent, a sort of unholy writhing, and her hands begin to tremble and she mutters to herself, "The man in black beckons. The man in black beckons. The man in black beckons."

Tyler leans toward her, snared by the pull of intrigue. He's forgotten to keep breathing. And as he leans, he blinks. But it's not the blink of an instant. It's the blink of time collapsing in on itself— top and bottom eyelids moving to meet each other like the march of a glacier to the shoreline. And the instant his eyelashes intersect, in a flash of light, Tyler sees the image of a little girl in pigtails. At first she's there and then she's gone. But her form again comes into view by the slow rise of dim backlighting from some unknown light source—perhaps it's simply the streetlight outside Dehlia's shop, casting shadows on the walls of Tyler's mind's eye—or perhaps it's some strange chemical reaction in his mind, the misfiring of neurons induced by stress and misplaced belief. The little girl stands before him, unmoving, unsmiling. Her skin is nearly translucent. Her neutral expression grows into a smile. A smile full of jagged, black teeth, like some undiscovered deep-sea creature. The image lingers in Tyler's mind's eye before fading into a silhouette of the girl's figure, gradually losing its form and spreading against the back of his eyelids like fog rolling across a glass lake.

Tyler opens his eyes and finds that he's nose-to-nose with Dehlia. She's become still and silent. Her closed eyes are calm. Neither of them moves. The tips of their noses brush together and they breathe each other in—as one exhales, the other inhales. Tyler hears the beating of his heart. And then the beating of her heart, slightly out of sync with his. The beating rises, faster and louder, until it crescendos into an unruly pounding of flesh and blood. Dehlia's face twitches and her eyes burst open—dark and empty. Tyler jerks back while breath flees his lungs.

"Your death will be in March."

Tyler sits motionless on the far side of the settee, eyes wide and mouth open as he watches Dehlia, nearly catatonic, steadily fill with life.

Once she fully recovers, an air of concern and regret emerges on her face and she lets her body slump. She tries to offer Tyler words of comfort.

"Like I said, the gift is not always reliable. It could be any March."

They sit in silence in the tiny parlor. Tyler retreats into himself.

Get out! Leave now!

But look at her ...

Those lips ...

Those eyes.

And if I'm going to die soon, I might as well get laid as much as possible.

Tyler emerges.

"Well, then. I guess I'll have to make the most of the next nine months."

Dehlia blurts out a nervous laugh. Tyler cracks a smile. They fall into an easy chuckle—a tacit acknowledgment that the ominous event is over and they should pick up where they left off when they first entered the shop.

9 YEARS LATER
Los Angeles, California

2

Siren.

An ambulance saunters down the street at the speed of caution, the sense of urgency in the blaring siren and flashing lights incompatible with the pace of travel. There's no need for the emergency medical technicians to drive with such an abundance of care at this late—or early—hour. The driver and his colleague simply lack enthusiasm for their work.

Having hurled himself to the floor upon hearing the approaching siren, Tyler lies facedown on the second story rooftop of a dimly lit strip mall. He's in the process of committing a number of crimes— and the evidence looms above him.

The decibel level plateaus as the ambulance slows to a crawl, searching for its nearby destination.

Shit. Is that for me?

Sounds like medics, not cops.

But if it IS the cops, and if they ARE here for me, they're gonna find me up here hugging the ground like a fuckin' dumbass.

Tyler grimaces.

Reflexes. After all these years … still gotta work on my reflexes.

The driver silences the wailing van. Blinking lights cast alternating red and orange hues on the surrounding structures. Friction from metal brake pad meeting metal rotor causes a sharp screech to penetrate the otherwise still night. Tyler's muscles involuntarily constrict as a survival instinct unsuccessfully attempts to draw his body closer to the ground—er, roof—beneath him. He turns his head over his shoulder and studies the variety of colors projected on a billboard protruding from the rooftop of the strip mall.

Red.

Orange.

Yellow.

No blue lights.

He lets out a terse sigh of relief.

No pigs … yet.

Tyler releases the tension in his body and makes his way toward the front edge of the rooftop, skeptical of what's happening on the street below. Bellying along the rough tar pitch, he winces as each coil and extension of his knees results in an audible scrape—the sound of someone tugging dead weight across a gravel road. He reaches the front of the building, lifts himself to one knee and peers over the short ledge of the building's façade.

Paramedics, indeed. Well, more like rent-a-medics.

Kitty-corner to the strip mall stands a brick apartment complex. An old man is wheeled out of the building on a gurney, an oxygen mask covering his face.

Poor old guy, I hope he makes it. Life's too short and no matter how long he's lived, I guarantee he didn't live enough.

A young girl trots out of the complex as the EMTs maneuver the gurney down the front steps. She's squeezed into a mini-skirt dress with semicircular cutouts that expose her midriff, and she struts in high heels and sports large hoop earrings—garden-variety club-rat gear. Curves in all the right places bounce as she springs down the steps of the building. She pauses on the sidewalk and looks back at the old man with a glimmer of concern.

Hmm, must be the old man's granddaughter.

As the gurney collapses into the back of the ambulance, a rotund, bull-legged woman totters onto the stoop, still dressed in a cook's uniform from a local late-night diner. She's in hysterics, sobbing and howling. *Must be the old man's wife.* She moves down the steps, clutching the handrail, taking them one at a time, all while spewing every manner of profanity in English and Spanish at the young girl, who starts to walk away from the scene.

That's no way to talk to your granddaughter. I didn't know grandmothers even knew those words. MY grandmother didn't know those words … at least, I don't think she did.

Upon reaching the sidewalk, the old woman waddles after the young girl. The young girl notices the attempted pursuit and lackadaisically picks up the pace. She's in no danger of being apprehended, despite tiny steps in tall heels.

The two generations migrate up the street and pass in front of the strip mall where Tyler watches from the rooftop. *Damn, that girl is FINE.* Visibly winded, the old woman abandons the chase and resumes the profane yelling.

"¡Sucia! Slut! ¡Ven aquí!" the old woman screams. "¡Te voy a matar, fucking puta!"

Geez, what did the granddaughter do?

The young girl spins around and faces the old woman, flashing a certain finger, one on each hand. The gesture inflames the old woman, who shrieks, slipping between languages, "If I see you again, seras en la ambulancia. ¡Puta! ¡Perra pendeja! Whore!"

"¡Atrévete!" the young girl finally retorts. "He wanted to play with a caja nueva. Must've been tired of your coño secada"—*Whoa, the granddaughter with the grandfather? Uh, something's not right*—"and apparently he got his money's worth! Fuck off, marrana!"

Ohhh, the granddaughter IS a whore … and, uh, probably not their granddaughter at all. THAT makes much more sense.

Ha, you old dog. You HAVE been living enough.

Feeling too exposed watching the drama play out from the mezzanine, Tyler creeps away from the ledge. But the old woman spots him before he's able to duck out of view. They lock eyes. *Oh no. Please, please be quiet.* And in that charming demeanor she shouts, "¿Qué coño estás mirando?"

Tyler freezes, hoping he's become invisible—another unsuccessful survival instinct. But the scream-fest continues.

"¡Oye! Hey you! ¡Estoy hablando con te en el techo!"

Having loaded the old man in the van and now mildly interested in the commotion up the street, the EMTs look toward the strip mall to see what the old woman is yelling at. They see Tyler, his head poking out just above the façade. His face illuminated by a red fluorescence emanating from the sign of a liquor store below him, named after that famed captain of the Nautilus, or a little lost clown fish. And in the reflection of the windows in the building across the street, Tyler stares at himself, his head just above that sign with a burned-out letter that now reads NEMO'_.

Shifting their gaze upward, the EMTs see what appears to be freshly painted graffiti on the outdated advertisement pasted in the billboard towering above Tyler. With dull eyes and lethargic expressions, the technicians do a slow double take. To Tyler, then to the graffiti. Tyler. Graffiti. One of them musters enough energy to say to the other, "I suppose we should call it in."

The jig is up. Tyler is quick to his feet and he gathers the tools of his trade: a half-used roll of duct tape, a flashlight, four stencils carved into thin cardboard, two cans of black spray paint and two cans of white. The stencils crumple as he stuffs each of the items into a duffle bag. *Dammit, those are ruined now.*

With a quick zip of the bag, he jets across the rooftop to his original point of entry and, fortunately, the ledge farthest from the EMTs. He drops the duffle bag to the ground where it lands in a damp alley between a dumpster and his bicycle. Grabbing hold of the metal safety cage that leads into the rooftop access ladder, Tyler turns his back to the alley and steps down into the hooped enclosure. When he emerges from the metal hoops, he decides to forgo the slow descent and let gravity do the rest. After all, this is what he's trained for, having spent many mornings over the years developing his climbing—and falling—skills at a local bouldering gym.

Moment of truth. He bends his knees, loosens his grip, leans back, and with short prayer he pushes himself from the ladder. The instant his fingers uncurl from the security of the metal rails, a pang of regret spears inside his gut. *Oh, fuck.* Practicing this basic maneuver in a controlled, indoor environment, falling onto a thick foam cushion, is one thing. Actually going through with it in the cold night when the stakes are high and the asphalt is the only thing to break your fall, is quite another.

Adrenaline surges into Tyler's bloodstream as if his adrenal medulla has projectile vomited after a long night of drinking.

Fuck, fuck, fuck.

The soles of Tyler's black Nike Air Pegasus greet the asphalt, and his muscles and joints negotiate the ratio with which each will absorb the force of impact. His thighs take the brunt of it, flexing to maximum capacity to terminate the downward momentum before thrusting Tyler into a backward somersault.

Tyler opens his eyes. He's suspended in a squatting position in the middle of the alley, the way one might look while taking a shit in the woods. In other words: a successful landing.

Praise Bacchus!

He bounds to his feet but loses his balance and stumbles, falling flat on his ass.

Goddammit.

Reflexes do not fail him this time. Simultaneous with the silent blaspheme he jumps up, slings the duffle bag over his shoulder and mounts his steed. In a matter of seconds, the old man, the foul-mouthed old woman, the fine young whore and the lifeless rent-a-medics are far behind him. He pedals through the streets of Los Angeles with reckless dexterity, never slowing in the face of yellow traffic lights, yielding to red lights only in the presence of intersecting headlamps.

Minutes later and a couple of miles traveled, Tyler eases on the pedals and lets the bicycle coast. As his velocity winds down, so does his body. Exhaustion sets in. Aforementioned adrenal medulla is empty and resting its head contentedly on the rim of a toilet seat where it will remain in the embrace of the porcelain throne until morning. He takes a deep breath and reflects upon the gravity—or levity—of recent events.

Damn. Close fucking call.

But in all my years catching tags, certainly I've been in greater danger of being caught. So why does tonight feel different? Why does tonight feel ... wrong?

It's been a while since I've had a run-in like that ... maybe I've forgotten what it feels like?

Maybe 'cause this is the first time I've had to run in my thirties?

'Cause with each throwie, the stakes get higher?

The City is always after me and if I'm ever caught, they'll have my hand ...

or my head. I know that. I've always known that and I accept the risk.

But this ... this feels ... different.

Is this finally the omen?

Tyler lets out a contemplative exhale.

No, of course not. I've been asking myself that question for too many years now.

But still ... maybe I should lay low for a while.

Tyler rolls into the parking lot of a gas station that boasts an "open all nite" mini-mart. The ride home will take another fifteen minutes and he figures he could benefit from a respite and replenishment of electrolytes. Tyler brakes near the mini-mart's automatic sliding doors and in one swift motion he dismounts and engages the kickstand. Duffle bag still slung across his body, he enters the mini-mart and heads toward the refrigerated beverages. He stands before the multitude of rehydration fluids and deliberates.

Red.

Orange.

Yellow.

No blue bottles.

He selects a color—er, flavor—proceeds to the counter and gives the clerk a few dollars. Without exchanging a word, the cashier taps a few buttons on the register, counts out coins from the tray and hands Tyler his change. Tyler swigs the yellow liquid and exits the mini-mart.

"Fuck!" Tyler hollers, frantically looking left and right.

His bike is nowhere to be found.

"Not again," he mutters, tilting his head back and swiveling it from side to side.

Bacchus, give me peace.

Tyler rummages through the duffle bag and pulls out a set of earbuds and an iPhone. He connects the earbuds to the device and scrolls through a catalogue of songs, searching for a tune to set the right mood for a long walk home.

Ah, perfect.

He presses his finger against the screen, which commences a magical sequence of events. A series of numbers stored on the device is accessed, decompressed, converted into sound waves, amplified, and delivered through tiny speakers resting delicately in the intertragic notch of each ear. There the sound is received and processed by an even more complex operating system. Synapses are stimulated, chemicals are secreted, and the sequence culminates in an emotional response evidenced by a universally understood manifestation: Tyler bobs his head.

In earlier recorded history, a device capable of a mere fraction of such wonder was reserved for only a select few—kings and queens, noblemen and sorcerers. In another age, those who employed such a contrivance were hunted and captured, accused of witchcraft, and burned at the stake. But in this modern era, the contraption is available for purchase by any commoner. Still, even today, some primitive civilization might worship the one who wields such a device. For what they cannot comprehend in the way of digital technology, they in turn may believe that a god dwells in the machine and that only the wielder can commune with him—or her. In any event, with the pressing of a finger against a screen, Tyler's disposition transmutes from that of frustration to that of tranquility—such wondrous alchemy.

Before Tyler leaves the gas station premises, he pulls a small marker from the pocket of his hoodie—a Molotow Masterpiece, loaded with black ink—and scribbles on the yellow posts that serve as crash barriers around the gas pumps. Then he slings the duffle bag over his shoulder and begins the long trek home.

Tyler walks the deserted streets entranced by Marco Polo's hypnotic beats. Masta Ace begins the first verse of the fifth track and Tyler rhymes along with him.

Just as the song reaches the chorus, Tyler is startled by the sight of something across the street. He pauses and stares in delighted disbelief, as if spotting an old friend across a cobblestone courtyard in a foreign city. There appears before him a forgotten bombing of his name—er, his municipal pseudonym. In big bubble letters on a cinderblock wall: SOBR.

Damn, it's been YEARS since I did that one. I can't believe it's still there. Tyler is filled with nostalgia and he beams with pride.

Man, graff is my life. I was born to get up on walls. If I'm ever caught, then so be it. I'll accept the punishment and be a martyr for the craft … and for the cause. I'll lead the rallying cry for writers and Insurrectionists everywhere. My anonymous comrades will bomb tribute pieces to me on every blank wall in every major city across the country. In SOBR we trust. Free SOBR. Shit, maybe another crew will start an online campaign to help with my legal costs.

Lay low for a while?

Nah.

Tyler takes a last look at the letters scribed in urban calligraphy on the dingy cinderblock canvas. He draws the hood of his sweatshirt over his head and walks on.

Rumble.

The knocking combustion of a diesel engine emerges from out of nowhere. Tiny explosions detonate and resonate through the piston cylinders of the engine block, rattling and guzzling—the inimitable warning of approaching authority.

Tyler stops dead in his tracks. He tosses the duffle bag behind a short hedge that separates a small parking lot from the sidewalk. He rushes over to a bus stop bench just a few paces away and he draws his hood low—appearing as just another down-on-his-luck Angeleno trying to survive the night. A chameleon blending into the background of the city's grungy tableau.

The sound grows louder and Tyler peers out from under the hood. Sweat gathers on his brow. A military Humvee rolls by— perhaps aimlessly, or perhaps with purpose. It doesn't matter. All that matters is that it's there and then it's gone.

It's been a while since I've seen one of those cruising the streets. Or maybe I've just gotten used to it. I suppose we all have.

Tyler fetches the duffle bag once the Humvee is long gone. He takes a few steps then pauses—is that more rumbling in the distance?

Fuck it, I'm gonna use Uber.

He retrieves that certain magic machine from the pocket of his jeans and waves his finger against the screen with graceful strokes and punctuated taps, like a conductor directing an orchestra, or a sorcerer performing chores.

A few minutes later, a car arrives and a stranger drives him home.

3

The chauffer halts the car in front of Tyler's house in the West Adams neighborhood of Los Angeles. Pleasantries are exchanged, but not currency. That is to say, neither bill nor coin is handed from one to the other. Rather, the gods who dwell in the pocket machines confer with each other and a collection of ones and zeros is offered by Tyler's god and accepted by the driver's god. The reparation is marked by a receipt that is sent to each person's electronic mailing address, and the monetary levels in their accounts reconcile accordingly.

Tyler stands on the front porch of the craftsman house, fumbling with his keys in the dark. *I've got to remember to turn on the fucking porch light before I fucking leave.* A shabby swing lies tilted on the porch—one end resting on the wooden floorboards, the other hanging by a twine of sisal rope. The house is teeming with life. A cockroach emerges from between the floorboards and scurries down the plank. Moths with folded wings walk along the wall. A nocturnal spider wraps its catch in a silky coffin. Tyler finally selects a key and inserts it in the knob of the perforated metal screen door. It doesn't quite fit. *Fuck.*

At last, Tyler unlocks the screen door and the interior door and steps into a small foyer. The instant the doors are closed and locked behind him, he drops the duffle bag to the floor and proceeds into the modest living room where the lights are dimmed low and his housemates are engaged in discussion.

"What, no television for you tonight? Thought you loved NatGeo at this hour," Tyler says with a jovial spirit.

They acknowledge him with their eyes, and one of them with a gesture that could possibly be construed as a nod, but they otherwise pay him no heed. They are engrossed in conversation as the one with black hair and a stern demeanor speaks without pause in some foreign accent. Tyler listens only briefly, as he lacks context and is weary from the events of the evening.

"So we start by acknowledging that there's a problem, numerous problems, which is what we've done here tonight—resource allocation, wealth disparity, corporate power, excessive consumption, to name a few. Then we need to acknowledge that, throughout history, more wickedness has been carried out by obeying the systems that enable these problems than by disobeying them. You and I, we are not inherently wicked. We are compliant or apathetic to the systems that carry out the ills all around us, which is to say that we are inherently complicit in the wickedness of others. To state it in the form of a cliché—if we are not part of the solution, then we are part of the problem. Well, I say no longer shall we be part of the problem. So, let us think now of solutions and the ways we should effectuate them."

Tyler furrows his brow and announces his departure. He walks down the hall to the back of the house, passing by photographs of memories of a more innocent time in life. Old friends. School photos. Vacations. His mother and father smiling in many of the photographs affixed to the walls, but no longer in the picture. A number of painted canvases and wood panels line the hallway floor. Some contain abandoned ideas, while others are current works-in-progress—each unfinished work representing a yet-to-be-fulfilled dream.

Tyler cracks open the door to his bedroom and immediately storms back into the living room.

"What the fuck, you guys? Seriously. What. The. Fuck? How did she get in here?" he demands. But his outrage and glare are returned with silence and downcast eyes.

"The back door was unlocked. She just waltzed right in," the stern one finally answers.

"And ..."

"And?"

"And you did nothing to stop her?"

"What could we do, push her back out the door?" the stern one asks.

Tyler's congenial housemate, the one with brown hair, mutters something unintelligible, which sounds vaguely like an apology.

"No, we won't be blamed for this," the stern one fires back.

Nothing to be done at this point and no sense in arguing, Tyler sneers and returns to the entrance of his bedroom.

Light from the living room spills into the hallway and races down the corridor but struggles to break into the bedroom and conquer the darkness therein. Tyler stands in the doorway and stares at the figure in his bed.

I suppose it's not completely awful, coming home to a naked woman asleep in my bed. But if she does this too often, she's gonna figure out how I spend my nights.

The door creaks as Tyler nudges it open just a little bit more. A shaft of muted orange light perforates the dark of the room and washes over the woman's brown and white spotted skin, causing her bare back to glow like an ember on the cusp of turning to ash.

Tyler closes the door behind him. He undresses and slips into bed in the spooning position.

"Hey," he says.

"Hey," she replies.

Slumber.

Tyler wakes to an empty bed—a balmy depression still imprinted in the mattress next to him. He shifts his eyes and glimpses Chloé's speckled back as she pulls a shirt down and over a sports bra. He stirs in bed, letting out an accentuated groan so that she'll realize he's awake.

"Morning," she says as she pulls up and ties off a pair of baggy sweatpants. "Was it a nice surprise, coming home to a warm bed?"

"Yeah, I guess so."

"You guess so? Well, I hope you don't think I was intruding. We only ever sleep at my place and you always leave in the middle of the night. It's been a few months and I just thought I would surprise you. Where were you anyway? Not that I'm asking in a jealous girlfriend kind of way, it's just that I was looking forward to seeing you and I waited around in your room—naked, I might add—and after a while I got worried and I didn't know if something happened to you and then I guess I just fell asl—"

"Video games at J's," Tyler interjects, to cease the sentence with no end in sight.

"Oh."

Chloé sits down on the edge of the mattress and slides on a pair of Reebok Atmos, the kind with the straps.

"Sorry I can't stick around this morning," she says. "Busy day. I'm teaching four classes and I have rehearsal tonight. And I have rehearsal all day tomorrow. You're going to Mollusk's opening Saturday night, right?"

"Am I going to the opening?" Tyler responds, contemptuously. "He's my mentor and this is a long-anticipated show. Of course I'm going Saturday night."

Chloé shoots a fleeting scowl at Tyler in response to the tone of his voice. "Good, then I'll meet you there." She leans over and kisses him, shoving her tongue in his mouth with playful aggression.

As she pulls away and stands up, Tyler smacks her ass—thick and round—and she squeals in mock disapproval.

"Saturday night," Tyler says in affirmation.

"Saturday night," she answers.

Chloé departs for the kitchen. Tyler departs for the shower.

Tyler dries himself and secures the towel around his waist. He hears Chloé's footsteps about the house and, finally, the opening and closing of the front doors. He stands in front of the mirror and admires his toned features before proceeding with his usual morning routine.

Knock-knock.

Okay, what did you forget?

Knock-knock.

Just let yourself in, the doors didn't lock behind you.

Knock. Knock.

"It's open!" Tyler yells to the front of the house.

Knock-knock-knock-knock-knock-knock-knock.

Fuck, alright already!

Still wearing only a towel, Tyler stomps to the front of the house and throws open the door while belting out, "You know the doors are unlo—"

"You need to fix your doorbell, dumbass."

"Faye! What the fuck are you doing here?" Tyler exclaims, poking his head outside, looking in all directions.

Faye tramps right past him and declares, "Don't worry, silly. I waited 'til she left. Watched her drive away and everything."

He hesitates before closing the doors, skeptical of her certainty. "Where did you park? Your car's not exactly subtle," Tyler says, referring to Faye's purple BMW convertible. "And exactly how long were you staking out my house?"

"Not long." Faye moves in close to Tyler and strokes the terrycloth bulge with the tip of her finger. "Just long enough to let the anticipation build. She has a great ass by the way. You're lucky."

"You can't just show up here like this."

"I know," she says, taking Tyler's hand and leading him back to his bedroom. "That's what makes it exciting."

To refer to Faye and Tyler as lovers would be to misappropriate the word. Love has no place in their recent acquaintanceship. Theirs is a mutual acknowledgement that each possesses the ability to satisfy the other's most primal desires—an affinity rooted in animal instinct, not enmeshed in emotion.

Faye pulls on the corner of the towel tucked under the fashioned waistband and Tyler lets it fall to the floor. They stand facing each other, motionless, reading each other's eyes to determine whether the next one who makes a move wins or loses, and what it might mean to win or lose in this rendezvous, and whether anything that follows could ever be regarded as losing.

Tyler heaves her to the bed and they fuck with equal parts vigor and apathy.

Tyler pulls out of Faye. They collapse and lie in silence, each meditating on the euphoric sensation that lingers after total satiation of lust and ecstatic swell of release. They do not spoon or cuddle or hold the hand of the other during this refractory period as lovers might. No, they lie apart. They are the most courteous of addicts—having derived pleasure from the plunge of a shared needle, of sorts—they respect the desire to privately savor the elixir of hormones and endorphins coursing through their bloodstream before the effect of the high dissipates completely.

Tyler comes to first. He doesn't move. He lies there and admires Faye's exposed body. He traces pale blue veins as they curve and splinter and disappear under colorful tattoos carved in her pasty white skin, like foreign continents spread across an alien atlas. He stares without blinking, an endeavor to etch this image in his memory forever—screen burn on the plasma display of his mind.

A moment later, Faye revives.

"And that's why we're playmates," she says, as she sits up and hunts for her various garments, not that there are many to find.

"Round two?"

"No," she says, with a hint of post-coital melancholy. "I wouldn't dare try to top that today." She hikes up a pair of denim cut-off shorts. "But I'll share a secret with you." She pauses and waits for Tyler to consent, which he does with the rolling gesture of a hand. "Lesley is showing your work in the upstairs gallery on Saturday night. It's supposed to be a surprise, so act surprised."

"Uh, okay. How do you know that?" Tyler says, his face wrinkled and serious.

"Oh, let's just say a little bird told me. You know she loves your work … and she thinks it will sell at this show. She's not at all disappointed it didn't do well last time."

"Again, how do you know that? Do you know Lesley?"

"Mmm, wouldn't you like to know," she says with mischievous inflection as she slips on a pair of wedge sandals. "I just thought I'd tell you, in case you weren't going to show up for some stupid reason."

"Well, I'll be there."

"Good. Maybe I'll see you there, maybe I won't."

"Maybe it would be best if you didn't."

"Oh, it's like that, is it?"

"You know it is."

"We'll see about that."

Faye sits down on the bed in the same spot Chloé sat minutes ago to strap on sneakers. She puts on a black and white polka dot halter top, the last piece of her scanty ensemble. Without warning, Faye's energy intensifies and a sudden, wild countenance renders her almost unrecognizable. She leans in close to Tyler and says, menacingly, "We may just be fucking around for now, you and I. But I know you. I know who you are. I know what you do. You're going to be famous one day, and I'm going to help you get there. Just remember that."

The two search each other's eyes to determine once more whether the next one who makes a move wins or loses.

After a prolonged interlude, Tyler says, "Alright, I'll remember."

"Good," she replies with a radiant smile and a cheery timbre, a stark contrast to her previous diction. She flips her long, vibrant red hair over her shoulder, bounds for the door and tenders a chipper, "See ya."

Tyler is left alone in his bed in that sort of awkward half-sitting-half-lying position, jaw agape, thunderstruck.

Uh, what the fuck just happened?

And what the fuck does she know?

Goddamn.

Tyler shrugs it off and sets about his day, a muggy December Thursday in Los Angeles. On the list of things to do: yoga, breakfast, doodle, cut new stencils, mix oils, buy a new bike, meet Isaiah for dinner, smoke a blunt, listen to records, go bombing.

Ah, but first he must cover his tracks. Tyler summons his god machine and initiates contact with Jason's pocket deity.

Silent J

-Yo if Chloe asks, we were
playing video games at your
place last night

-Got it

                              -Thanks

-Word

4

Tyler pedals at top speed, duffle bag in tow. The streets at this time of night are devoid of activity and so he helms the bike with a certain degree of abandon. Streetlamps, bus stops and civic foliage flit past him and the nighttime skyline fluctuates as he steers toward his destination.

He veers left and the top edge of it peeks out in the distance. He spies it with salacious intent as it exposes itself to him, growing larger with each rotation of the pedal crank until the entire surface area is in plain view.

Tyler squeezes the brake lever and skids to a stop. He straddles the bicycle in the middle of the street—left foot on the ground, right foot on the pedal at the pinnacle of its orbit, hands in his lap, breath heavy. He stares at the grand panel with the same determination that the Italian Renaissance sculptors once trained upon blocks of unformed marble.

Floating above the parking lot of a national pharmacy chain is a fourteen-by-forty-eight-foot billboard shining against the dark sky. It's not unlike the object of Tyler's bombing last night, except this billboard resides at an intersection heavily travelled by the Los

Angeles proletariat during the drudge of the workday commute. Framed therein is an advertisement that heralds the upcoming semi-annual sale of a low-end clothing retailer. The image portrays a slender woman lounging in this season's new coat and blue jeans. Her sparkling eyes and perfect smile emote the requisite amount of glee that the marketers want the casual onlooker to associate with their company's brand. And the slogan cheerfully suggests—or desperately begs—in big block letters, "Spend more on you!"

Product advertising is the nationalist propaganda of a capitalist society. Instead of "Your country needs you!" the slogans read "You need these!" Instead of "Workers of the world unite!" the masters command "Workers of the world go buy!" Brand marketers employ the same psychological mechanisms of influence and persuasion in these public proclamations as a fascist regime, except the desired result is not to inspire a young soul to forge fidelity to their country, but to conspire to separate a poor soul from their money.

Tyler guffaws and shakes his head with incredulity at the audacity of the message.

The slogan actually says 'Spend, moron you!'

Drive on, work hard, then give us your money, you men and women of labor ... and remember that you too can be this happy in a pair of our jeans.

Tyler grins to himself when he sees that the light blue background and the bountiful negative space in the advertisement will afford him a good measure of artistic freedom.

It's the marketer's aim to place an advertisement wherever they think it will make an impression—newspapers, magazines, television, the Internet. And just when you think you can escape the clasp of the marketer's influence by setting down the paper or turning off the screen, you walk outside only to find that their mark is inescapably all around you—on buses, at bus stops, along highways, on the temporary fencing at construction sites, in billboards towering above intersections and even streaming behind a fixed-wing airplane during an otherwise serene day at the beach.

For where your attention is, there an ad will be also.

In this regard, the graffiti writer is no different than the marketer. They want to be seen, to be known, to leave an impression. But instead of placing ads, they catch tags. Graffiti writers compete with each other to cover the city with their scribbles and missives—to get up and stay up everywhere—on buses, at bus stops, along highways, on the temporary fencing at construction sites, in billboards towering above intersections and, yes, even streaming behind a fixed-wing airplane at the beach. And graffiti writers might argue that defacing billboards is their right as residents of the city who did not consent to allowing marketers to pollute the skyline with sales pitches. "If the marketers can erect their signs, then we can write our names," they might say. But the average resident has given no such consent to either the marketer or the graffiti writer. Thus, the act of graffiti is as much a form of hypocrisy as it is protest, or civil disobedience, or counterpropaganda—or whatever other lofty ideal they confer to it.

As to which is more aesthetically pleasing, the ad or the graffiti, that's a matter of personal opinion. But if we are to weigh the ills of the ubiquity of outdoor advertising against the inevitable presence of graffiti in The Big City, it's incumbent upon us to remember that one group's motivation is manipulative in nature—intended to alter our purchasing behavior, demanding that we conform and swear allegiance to a particular brand. Whereas the other group's motivation is expressive in nature—intended to remind us that they are alive and out there, seizing the night and declaring "Damn the Man!" And in the heart of even the most stodgy, straitlaced person, deep down, a small part of them wishes they could join ranks with this second group—perhaps not to tag walls or to vandalize property, but to live as fearlessly and freely.

Tyler cycles into the parking lot and stashes the bike in the cranny formed between a robust grouping of foxtail weeds and a bulky electric power box in the back alley near the loading bays. He slides on a pair of tight, leather gloves, fastens the Velcro strap around his wrist, and jogs to the circular base of the thick metal mast that buttresses the heraldic sign. His senses are on high alert. His eyes dart to every flicker of city light and his ears filter the hum of city night, scanning for the sound of footsteps and diesel engines. He stands under the commercial obelisk with his head tilted back as he mentally rehearses the plan of attack.

The ladder looks to be in good shape.
The panel down here is sturdy.
Both should hold the rope just fine.
Bottom rung is about twenty, maybe twenty-five feet up ... not too bad.

The lights are still on. I'll need to take care of them right away.

This shouldn't be too difficult. I'll be very exposed, even at this hour. But I suppose that's what draws me to it.

After a double- and triple-check of his surroundings, Tyler commences Phase One of the siege: Set up. From the duffle bag he retrieves a nylon climbing rope with one end attached to a clunky D-shape carabiner. He holds the coiled rope like a lasso and swings the carabiner in wide vertical circles, building momentum with each revolution before releasing it high into the air to loop it between two rungs of the ladder suspended above him. One revolution … two revolution … three … release!

He misses.

The carabiner falls to the concrete with a dull clank.

Tyler swivels his head to look over each shoulder. He's not at the stage of the mission where he's in much danger of being caught, but better to be safe than sorry. Right now, to the average passerby, he's just a man standing in a parking lot under a billboard with a duffle bag (filled with illicit items) at one in the morning. That's not such an uncommon sight in Los Angeles. The rope is a curious element, but most Angelenos would rather not get involved—ask no questions, give no fucks—at least not yet.

Tyler pulls the carabineer back to him and tries again. One … two … three … release! The carabiner flies between the second and third lowest rungs and dangles on the other side of the ladder. *Praise Bacchus!* And now he must act quickly, because now he's a man standing in a parking lot, under a billboard, with a duffle bag (filled with illicit items) at one in the morning, with a rope dangling from the ladder above him—this scene is reasonably suspicious.

Tyler slacks and feeds the nylon climbing rope so that the carabineer drops down to him. He hooks the carabineer to the end of a sisal rope that has large, evenly spaced knots tied throughout. He raises the knotted rope to the metal rungs of the ladder, then he wraps the other end of the nylon rope around the great mast once, twice and another loop around, each time circling just underneath the electric panelboard, utilizing it as a holdfast. He ties off the climbing rope and tests the capacity of the rope ladder by pulling down on one of the knots with all of his might. The nylon rope draws taught and the rope ladder proves secure.

Phase Two: Ascension. Tyler slings the shoulder strap of the duffle bag around his torso so that the bag sits low on his back. Both hands grab at a knot just above his head and aforementioned adrenal medulla starts to gag. He lifts his knees to his abdomen and clenches a knot between his feet. As he pushes himself up with his legs, his hands walk the rope one over the other to grasp the next knot. Again, he lifts his knees to his abdomen, clenches a knot, pushes up, hands walk the rope, and so on. And now he's a man in a parking lot, with a duffle bag (filled with illicit items) at one in the morning, swinging from a rope under a billboard like Errol Flynn in some goddamn urban swashbuckler film.

Tyler soon reaches the top of the knotted rope. He grabs the bottom rung of the ladder and begins to climb. Once his feet are secure on the bottom rung, he dips down and pulls out a small carabineer fastened to his ankle by a short cord. He latches the ankle-carabineer to the knotted rope and unlatches the knotted rope from the nylon rope, letting the nylon rope fall to the ground. He drags the knotted rope behind him as he climbs, swinging his leg far from the ladder while stepping up so that the knots don't catch on any of the rungs.

Tyler reaches the top of the access ladder and hoists himself onto the catwalk. He sits on metal grille, letting his feet dangle over the precipice. He grabs hold of the knotted rope at his ankle, unlatches it from the carabineer and reels it up, coiling it along the way before placing it back in the duffle bag. And now he's a man sitting on the catwalk of a billboard, still with a duffle bag (still filled with illicit items), still in the second hour of the morning, but with nothing dangling from the billboard—just a rope laying at the base of the mast, hardly noticeable among the litter on the dirty sidewalk. The most difficult part of the siege is over, but there's still one more phase before he can get to work.

Phase Three: Blackout. The billboard is lit from below by two floodlights that jet out from the walkway. Tyler retrieves two thick, black canvas sacks from the duffle bag and scurries along the catwalk, hooding each light. The billboard goes dark and Tyler is at ease.

This is what earns Tyler—er, SOBR—the honor of being one of the most respected and notorious graffiti writers in Los Angeles—

named alongside the likes of CHAKA, AYER, GKAE, DREAM, SABER and JOSEY. These daring writers risk imprisonment, fines, injury and even their lives to reach the otherwise inaccessible public platforms—the heavenly spots—to exhibit their work. In this way, their work can be short and simple, for it is the combination of illegality and daring placement that lends the tag, the throwie, the piece—and in this case, the message—its power, not haughty prose. And the degree of difficulty for the writer in accessing a chosen location is directly proportional to the level of effort required to restore the defaced surface. Thus, these prestigious few are lauded by their contemporaries, loathed by property owners and continuously pursued by The City.

Tyler fetches the modest tools of his trade for this particular evening: two cans of white spray paint, one can of black and one red. He shakes the pressurized canister of white paint and it makes the clink-clang-clink sound of ball bearings banging around the tin wall. He presses down on the plastic actuator cap with his index finger. This action opens a spring-loaded valve at the top of the canister, which reduces the air pressure inside the can, causing a propellant mixture and the liquid pigment to feed through a dip tube and expel out of the plastic nozzle in a fine mist and with a cathartic hiss.

With body-length strokes and circular motions, Tyler paints a crude outline of his composition—referred to by the graff community as a throw-up, or a "throwie." Once the outline is in place, he fishes in his pockets for a different set of actuator caps— fat caps—designed to spray a wide field of paint. He fits the fat caps on both cans of white paint, and with one can in each hand he fills in the crude outline in a dual spray action, each hand moving back-and-forth, meeting at his sternum and deployed outward—a technique that allows him to quickly fill in the entire body of the throwie. Time is always of the essence to the graffiti writer. After the body is filled in, Tyler uses the black spray paint to trace back over the outline, giving the throwie shape and definition, forming the bubbled letters and the symbol therein. This final outline is finished in a manner of seconds and, as a final touch, Tyler tags his moniker in red paint—ratifying his iconoclastic declaration with the ink of an aerosol quill. He steps back and basks in the satisfaction of a job well done.

In penning a featurette for a weekly city magazine, a culture columnist might be inclined to refer to graffiti as a "lifestyle." And while that term may be fitting in reference to the casual graffiti writer—the toys, the unattended rich kids with no sense of purpose—for the masters of the craft, the term is entirely inapt. To the masters—the kings, the queens—graffiti far transcends the diminishing suffix. To them, graffiti is breath. It's bread and water. It's spirit and soul. Meditation. Reason and desire. It is simply "life." The only "style" about it is in the unique form of lettering.

And so it is for Tyler—his selfhood inextricably intertwined with his anonymous identity in a double helix of blood and paint. As the hoarder is compelled to amass unsalable effects, as the kleptomaniac is compelled to pocket meaningless trinkets, as the nymphomaniac is compelled to fuck, Tyler is compelled to go out night after night painting the town red—and black, and white, and whichever other color he has with him. Graffiti is his anti-drug—or it's a sunny-side-up egg sizzling in his cast iron skull.

Crackle.

A few moments after scribbling his sigil, Tyler's ears pick up on the soft crunch of rubber on asphalt. His stomach sinks and it momentarily takes his breath with it. He stands fear-frozen on the walkway.

Reflexes—what say you? Probably best not to stay standing, dumbass.

Tyler crouches and scuttles to the farthest end of platform and lies down on the metal grate. He inches out a little farther so he can peer under and around the billboard.

But curiosity is what got you in trouble last night …

Ah, fuck it.

A black Cadillac Escalade pulls into the alley behind the drugstore. It stops adjacent to the bulky electric power box where Tyler stashed his bike. The driver leaves the engine running and scoots out of the car. The driver is a moving mass, a looming shadow dressed all in black with leather gloves and a ski mask—a big motherfucker, this one.

Shiiit, this looks bad, man. This looks really bad.

The silhouetted figure walks to the back of the vehicle and opens the cargo hatch door. It tugs on an object in the rear bay of the car and lets the object fall to the asphalt with a thud. It rolls the object over with a gruff kick and from high above Tyler sees the bashed and bloody face of a dead man.

Tyler jolts backward and his foot knocks over the canister of red paint. He winces as he looks behind to see the canister rolling and curving toward the edge of the catwalk. *No, no, no. Please stop!* The canister slows and teeters, half on the walkway, half suspended in air. *Praise Bacch—Oh, shit!* The canister tips over the edge and Tyler closes his eyes as it falls in seemingly slow motion and hits the ground with what may as well be the sound of a mortar on a battlefield.

The shadowy figure jerks in the direction of the canister and looks up at the billboard. It cocks its head to one side and struts over to the drop-site. With the canister spinning between its feet, the black mass looks directly at Tyler. It bends down and picks up the canister, twirls it in the air and catches it with one hand. Tyler watches in horror as the figure walks back to the body, sprays the dead man's face with red paint and heaves the corpse into a pile of cardboard and plastic trash next to a dumpster in the alley. It tosses the spray can in the dumpster, returns to the vehicle and drives away.

Tyler's adrenal medulla evacuates all contents and blacks out for the night.

Phase Four: Panic.

What the fuck?

What the fuck!

I gotta get outta here! NOW!

Tyler uncovers the floodlights and stuffs the remaining canisters in the duffle bag. He drops the duffle to the sidewalk and starts down the access ladder. There's no time to bother with erecting the mechanism he would ordinarily use to repel down the steel monolith. For all he knows, the driver could soon return to the scene, as an afterthought, to leave no witness. Or the police could already be in close pursuit of the driver, in which case they would find Tyler with his name—that notorious street pseudonym—freshly scribed in the same red paint that now adorns the face of a dead man. And this being LA, he knows all too well that the pigs are likely to shoot first and ask questions later. So, no. There is no repelling tonight. Once again, there is the immutable assistance of gravity.

Tyler dangles from the bottom rung of the ladder and beseeches his lord and savior.

Bakkhos Perikionios, hear my prayer. By thy unyielding power render this vessel indestructible. Bless me, your devoted supplicant, as I fall. Forgive my iniquity and deliver me free from injury. In thy glory and thy name, amen.

Tyler releases and plummets.

And somewhere in Los Angeles, a lone maenad twerks before an audience of lecherous satyrs.

The First Hymn.

The choir is gathered on the stage inside the candlelit sanctuary and there's a friendly murmur of greetings and well-wishes. The chatter dies down as the choir members begin vocal exercises. Each member warms their vocal cords by oscillating through the breadth of their pitch. The resulting chaotic resonance is a thing of dread and beauty, reminiscent of "Requiem" by György Ligeti. The vocal exercises conclude after a couple of minutes and the choir members don hideous masks and draw the hoods of their cowls. Silence falls over the chamber. Contorted faces stare blankly at the parishioners seated in the pews. Someone must have given a cue, because the chorus bursts into song in sudden and perfect unison.

Praise him! Father Bacchus, from whom all blessings stem
Praise him! Eleutherios, liberator of men
VoHé! VoHé! Again we cry VoHé!
We find forgiveness in Dionysus, he hears us when we call
We know victory in Aesymnetes, he saves us when we fall
O brothers! We gather in his name, to rejoice and partake of
restoring wine
O sisters! We dance and sing and rave, in the holy hills our secret
rites enshrined
Praise him! Father Bacchus, from whom all blessings stem
Praise him! Eleutherios, liberator of men
VoHé! VoHé! Again we cry VoHé!

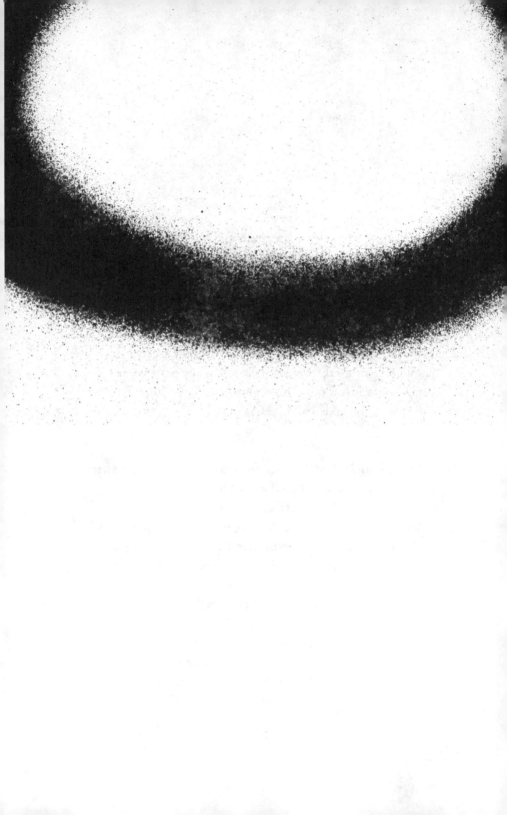

5

The two a.m. worship service is underway. Tyler enters the sanctuary of The Eternal Church of the Bakkheia as the first hymn draws to a close. He takes a seat in a pew in the back of the chamber as the second hymn begins. The congregation is scattered throughout the room. All are free to worship as they please. Some stand and dance and shout while the choir sings. Others kneel with heads bowed, mumbling the lyrics or chanting personal invocations.

Tyler sits nearly catatonic in the pew—a tired and sweaty mess. His thoughts are fragmented and incoherent. He's not in control of them as they weave between prayer and reconciliation in a fit of traumatic stress.

... what was that? what the fuck was that? ... I'm sorry ... I'm so sorry ... Bacchus, hear my voice ... please forgive me ... amen ... he's dead ... that guy's dead ... what do I do ... what did I do? ... I killed a man ... no ... yes, I killed a man ... no, I didn't do anything ... the man in black did it ... thank you for saving me ... thank you for keeping me safe ... amen ... oh, man ... I'm in trouble ... I'm in big trouble ... I didn't do anything ... I was just tagging ... shit ... the pigs are gonna see my name ... they're gonna come looking for me ... for SOBR ... maybe that's what they wanted ... Bacchus ...

help me ... please help me ... amen ... oh, man, I'm so fucked ... so, so fucked ... I need strength ... give me strength ... amen ... Tyler's head twitches as the image of a little girl with jagged black teeth flashes in his mind ... *Bacchus give me guidance and wisdom ... amen ... be my shepherd ... watch over me ... strike my enemies down with the blow of your thyrsus ... amen ... love me as you love your beloved beasts ... care for me as you care for the panther ... give me the strength of your tiger ... and the cunning of your leopard ... omen ... lead me down the path of righteousness ... keep my cup running over with your wine ... omen ... omen? ... last night ... last night was an omen ... it was a warning ... it was thee omen ...* dark teeth like razors from behind tender pink lips form a wily smile in Tyler's mind's eye *... I should've laid low ... I shouldn't've gone bombing tonight ... the omen ... someone did this to me ... someone's coming for me ... the man in black ... the man in black beckons ... and now they'll come for me ... I was set up ... framed ... oh, god ... I've been framed.*

The fourth hymn dwindles to a slow, repetitive intonation—a light polyphonic melody from one of the female choir members. Tyler stands up, still shaken, but ready to ride home.

Unbeknownst to Tyler, two worshipers had arrived and sat next to him during his trance. The female worshiper wears a blue and white toga with a red sash slung around her shoulder in a manner such that one breast is exposed. The male is shirtless—a garment fashioned from purple cloth and leopard skin draped around his waist. Tyler begs their pardon as he passes by. The male parishioner, perhaps sensing a troubled stirring in Tyler's soul, stands and places his hand on Tyler's shoulder. Tyler pauses and turns toward him. He takes Tyler's face gently into his hands, kisses Tyler on the mouth and says, "VoHé, son." Tyler returns the gesture with a solemn nod of gratitude and whispers, "VoHé." The man remains standing and watches Tyler shuffle toward the aisle.

At the credence table in the back of the chamber, Tyler ladles a small glass of wine from an ancient krater into a communal kantharos crafted in the form of a satyr. He pours a small amount of the wine into a spittoon in honor of Bacchus and fallen friends, then swigs the rest.

Tyler draws the magic machine from his pocket and initiates a payment application. A barcode appears on the screen and he flashes it in front of a point-of-sale scanner set up at the holy table.

A message pops up on the screen: Thank you for your tithe. It has been 1 year, 1 month and 6 days since your last visit.

Tyler wrinkles his face at the thought of having missed services for so long. But his tithe is accepted and he feels rested, which is all that matters at the moment. He exits the sanctuary just as the fifth and final song begins.

Tyler walks his bicycle up the driveway and parks it in the backyard. Dried leaves crunch under light footsteps somewhere behind him. His spine stiffens and out of nowhere a cat rushes past him and enters the house through a large doggy door. He lets out a sigh and shakes his head. *Fuckin' cat.* He pulls the can of red spray paint from his duffle bag—having retrieved it from the dumpster before fleeing the scene. *Now what do I do with this?* He hesitates before nonchalantly tossing it in his city-issued recycling bin. It clangs in the bin and settles among many dozens of canisters just like it.

Keys in hand, Tyler shuffles up the steps to his back door. Before inserting the key, he grabs hold of the doorknob and twists it with a twinge of apprehension. *Fuck. Unlocked. This is no time for a visitor.* He walks into the kitchen and rummages for a snack while eavesdropping on his housemates and a few of their guests, who are once again engaged in late night discourse in the living room. The stern one leads the discussion while sitting on the armrest of the sofa—the whole scene looks like some strange form of discipleship.

"What are the potential solutions? Rewrite history books? Reinvent languages? Reform education curricula? Regulate industries? Remodel economic systems? Revolutionize governments? Restructure societies? The list goes on—pick your poison.

"What are the tools to accomplish any of this? Get organized? Raise awareness? Boycott? Strike? Lobby? Sway the hearts and minds of men and women? Whatever the means may be, the best place to start is right here, at home—this city, this neighborhood. But if someone was to speak up, would anyone listen? I'm afraid to say it, but I don't think they would.

"You see, Americans have become largely oblivious—unconsciously or willfully—to the ills caused by their systems. How? Why? Maybe it's because their standard of living is so tremendously high—maybe it's been so high for so long that they've forgotten the sense of fear and desperation that comes with the everyday struggle for survival. Or maybe they have not forgotten—maybe they remember and they simply do not care. For as long as their current way of life is not markedly diminished, then, to them, the systems are working properly, and all is right in the world. Indulge me for a moment—

"I believe that the American spirit has been soiled by convenience and an abundance of choice. Convenience—instant access, immediate results, the general lack of struggle—has made Americans largely ignorant and lazy. Choice—the vast array of selection, options, configurations—has stunned them with a barrage of superficial decisions to be made on a daily basis. Convenience and Choice have nurtured a culture of instant and selfish gratification— what I want, when I want it, where I want it, how I want it; the customer is always right; fast food; microwaves; 3D printing; social media; regular, diet, zero; megabyte, gigabyte, terabyte; harder, better, faster, stronger. And make no mistake, this culture of instant and selfish gratification transcends youth—it has become as much a quality of the old as that of the young. This culture is engrained in them. They're addicted to it—sedated by it. It occupies their mind and it dictates how they spend their time. Consequently, it's where the core of their values lies. As long as their way of life remains unthreatened, as long as the individual can indulge in the pleasure of Choice at their whim and the individual otherwise lives Conveniently, the American people will remain compliant or apathetic to the systems imposed upon them by their masters—just look at how they let a president become a king. And they care not of the long-term effects of the systems or the residual harm that may affect a disenfranchised minority or an outsider. Selfish wants come first and the needs of others second … or third … or sometime down the line, whenever it's convenient.

"Population control in this sort of manner is not a novel concept. Bread and Circus have long been used to placate and distract a populace. The difference here is that Convenience and Choice have gone a step beyond merely placating and distracting the American people—these conventions have fleeced them of altruism and solidarity.

"Sure, at times some may raise their voice—shouting of the injustices of the systems. Some may occupy city parks in peaceful demonstration. Some may write or sing of revolution. Some may even run for office, desperate to engage the public in a national discussion. These are the exceptional few. When it comes to galvanizing the masses and effectuating action, Americans are conspicuously absent. Not until at least one of these conventions is threatened—Convenience or Choice—will Americans truly be motivated to engage. 'Give me Convenience or give me death!' they will chant. 'Freedom of Choice!' they will shout … perhaps while tossing crates of imported electronics into a harbor.

"Now, I make this assessment of the current state of the American consciousness in sweepingly general terms, crudely formulated and supported only by my plain observation, and perhaps you think I'm being unfair—unfair in the oversimplification, or unfair that I'm singling out our current homeland. But I make the assessment, such as it is, with the belief that it applies to many nations with equal measure. That is to say, this is not just an American epidemic, but a pandemic of humankind."

Heads nod in contemplation—wheels turn therein.

Tyler peeks around the doorway to his bedroom. The room is empty and he sighs in relief—or is it disappointment? He collapses to the bed, fully clothed, and succumbs to sleep the instant his cheek touches the cool comfort of the pillow.

6

Ring. Buzz.

Tyler is jarred awake by the sound of a cheery marimba-like ringtone. The machine in his pocket vibrates and falls silent. He lies with wide-open eyes as his body and mind revive. Again, the machine rings, vibrates and falls silent. A moment later it proffers a series of delicate pings. Tyler reluctantly submits to its beckon and swipes his finger across the screen.

Silent J

-Get your ass to the bar
-Izzy will meet us here
-I'm fucking serious. Get over
here NOW

Damn, chill the fuck out, J. What's got you so worked up?

Tyler yawns and stretches his arms and legs against the bedsheets like a snow angel, or the Vitruvian Man.

A'ight. I'll head over ...

Soon.

Tyler proceeds with his usual morning—er, afternoon—routine before heading to the bar.

Tyler parks his truck in front of Nowhere, a saloon that straddles the border of Los Angeles and Culver City. The interior of the tavern is a hodgepodge of French bordello décor, vaudevillian motif, and hip-hop and punk rock paraphernalia. The windowless walls are plastered with *toile de Jouy*. Crystal chandeliers equipped with red and orange light bulbs hang throughout the room. Portraits of classic movie monsters and subculture icons are sheathed in Victorian picture frames and lit by gaudy sconces. Two pool tables sit in the back of the bar. Ornate chairs and sofas and tufted booths offer plenty of seating options. Flat screen monitors cycle through cult-classic films with the volume on mute.

The drinkery is a refuge for various non-conformist subcultures. All those who are open-minded are welcome to gather and socialize outside the comfort of their usual coterie. After all, gutter punks and backpackers, goths and rudies, greasers and metalheads and, yes, even Juggalos and hippies, are all united by the same fundamental "fuck the world" tenets—their differences are merely a matter of aesthetics. And in such uneasy times, these societal factions grow united evermore by the talk of dissent and the whispers of insurrection. Even some straight-edgers frequent the bar—for the camaraderie and political discourse, not the drink specials.

The most beloved feature of the tavern is a small stage in the corner of the side room. A microphone clasped at the top of a thin, chrome mic stand is positioned at center stage. Every night is "open mic night" at Nowhere and all are free to express themselves. The rules, posted on the wall next to the stage, are simple: 1. No hate speech. 2. All patrons must be respectful of the speaker and vice versa. 3. The manager on duty has complete discretion to cut the mic on anyone, for any reason whatsoever. (Ah, the irony that such a fascist principle would exist in such a liberal haven.)

As one might expect, the stage is often occupied by nervous people performing awful poetry or sophomoric stand-up comedy, or reading an ill-conceived short story. But even if the performance is not appreciated, the courage is admired. However, every once in a while, someone takes the stage and leaves the crowd awestruck, like they just witnessed an early performance by Bob Dylan or Tupac Shakur.

Tyler enters the bar. It's mid-afternoon on a Friday—the quiet before the weekend storm—just the faint clacking of billiard balls in the background and the moody crooning of Nick Cave on the jukebox. Tyler is greeted by the proprietor of Nowhere.

"Where the fuck have you been?" Jason demands.

"Sleeping … until you woke me up."

"Why didn't you text me back?"

"I … you didn't ask a question. I got your texts and came over."

"You took your sweet-ass time doing so."

Tyler shrugs.

"Ay, cabrón estúpido, sit the fuck down. Have you seen the news, yet?"

Tyler pauses before slowly uttering, "No."

"Well, here ya go."

Jason starts the digital feed of an NBC news bulletin that had been paused on a monitor above the bar. A woman with big hair and too much make-up introduces the story.

BREAKING NEWS THIS AFTERNOON as authorities announce a county-wide search for a graffiti vandal known by the moniker S-O-B-R or simply as "sober". *Oh, man. This is not good.* The announcement follows the discovery of a body behind a pharmacy in South Central Los Angeles this morning. We go now to Brack Stone who is live *What a stupid name.* on the scene with the story.

Thank you, Sandra. Police have yet to identify the body of a man found dead in the alley behind this CVS earlier this morning. But authorities now have reason to believe that local graffiti vandal, SOBR, is connected with the incident. What was thought to be dried blood on the face of the deceased has now been identified as being a combination of blood and red spray paint. And now as we zoom out, you will notice the defacement of the billboard above the drugstore parking lot—and, my apologies, we have to blur the words for you viewers at home, but you'll get the gist of it. Now, as you can see, the words "'blank' the king" appear with an upside down crown dotting the "i" in the word "king", and the vandal's moniker tagged on the lower right side of the piece. Local residents and CVS employees confirm that the vandal's work was not on the billboard yesterday, leading police to believe that the mystery man, or woman, behind the SOBR alias may have witnessed, or may be directly involved in, the incident that took place last night. Police have not commented on whether SOBR is a suspect in the murder but have simply stated that the vandal is a person of interest. Of course, SOBR remains at large for longstanding crimes against property in LA and surrounding counties and, now, perhaps for crimes against The Crown. Brack Stone reporting live in South

Shiiit.

Pleased with himself, a smile emerges on Tyler's face. *Nice. Glad the piece looks good from the street.*

Goddammit.

Tyler takes a deep breath and nods

Central Los Angeles. Sandra, back to you in the studio.

Thank you, Brack. SOBR is known to property owners and authorities as the "Scourge of the Southland." The elusive vandal has been terrorizing property for as long as eleven years according to JoAnne Collins, Director of the Office of Community Beauti—

his head in reluctant acceptance of his situation.

Ha, it's been a lot longer than that.

Jason stops the footage. "Seen enough?"

"Yeah. Listen. I wasn't invol—"

"Save it. I want Isaiah to be here when you tell the story of this completely fucked up situation."

Jason pours Tyler a beer and Tyler takes it over to one of the pool tables. In his opening turn he sinks the five ball and scratches on the two.

Tyler finds his way back to a barstool after a couple of hours shooting pool. The population of the tavern has grown, and he passes time by people-watching.

A gorgeous blonde girl hurries into the bar and takes station behind the counter. Tyler casts a sideways glance at Jason. Jason glares back at Tyler, shaking his head in disapproval. When the girl is out of earshot, Jason says, "She's new and she's proving to be a good bartender. I don't want her getting mixed up in your shit. Off. Limits."

Tyler grimaces, then nods in grudging acknowledgement of Jason's wish.

A sudden chill runs up Tyler's spine and slivers through his arms and legs.

The front door opens and Isaiah enters Nowhere. Then again, Isaiah exudes such charisma that his presence is often sensed by his friends prior to his arrival, and so it would be more accurate to say that Isaiah's spirit enters Nowhere and his body follows close behind. Isaiah quickly spots Tyler and beelines toward him.

"Well ain't you in some shit."

"C'mon Izzy, you know I had nothing to do with—"

"Yeah, I figured as much. I've been dealing with it all day. Now explain what happened."

Tyler responds in a hushed tone, "Shouldn't we go somewhere a little more … private?"

"No, we're gonna do it right here, right now, motherfucker."

Isaiah sits on the stool next to Tyler, the glow of the red and orange lights reflects off his dark, bald head. Jason leans in with one elbow propped up on the counter, his fist tucked under a wispy goatee. Tyler recounts the events of the prior night in mind-numbing detail and Isaiah interrupts with precisely worded questions throughout the account. Tyler ends the interrogation by telling them the conclusion he reached during his trance at the sanctuary, which humors Isaiah.

"Ha! Framed? You narcissistic motherfucker, you're not being framed. This is real life, not the movies. There's no conspiracy, there's no nefarious plot here. The fact of the matter is that the ski-mask-wearing-motherfucker would have never seen you had the canister not rolled off the platform. You were just in the wrong place at the wrong time and *you* fucked up."

Fuck you, Izzy. "Well, I disagree."

"Oh, you do, do you? Who's framing you then?"

"I don't know … uh—"

"Who, Tyler?"

"Uh—"

"Who!"

"I don't know! Maybe a writer who's got beef with me? A crew? A gang? Loyalists … anyone who's discovered my identity!"

"Discovered your identity? Now that's interesting. Other than me and J, who the fuck knows that you're"—Isaiah pauses and remembers that they're in a public forum. He composes himself and rephrases the question—"knows who you are?"

The question catches Tyler off-guard. He had raddled off an answer to support his theory without really thinking about it. Forced to consider the possibility that the secret of his identity extends beyond the threesome, he zones out in that way people do when thinking about nothing at all or everything at once. His pupils dilate and flashes of indiscretion flood his mind.

I've been careless lately … left the duffle bag in the foyer … the backdoor is always unlocked … my piece book is laying around somewhere … apparently Chloé comes and goes as she pleases … Faye said she knows who I am, what the fuck does that mean? … Oh shit, and I told Mollusk about a year ago.

Tyler's pupils contract as he snaps back to reality and answers Isaiah's question.

"Nobody. I've been careful."

But Tyler had been absent for a moment too long.

"Nobody? You're lying."

"Fuck you, Izzy. I don't need this shit from you. You guys haven't been catching tags in, what, a decade?" He admonishes Isaiah, "You left the life to patrol the streets." He chides Jason, "You traded writing on street walls for working on Wall Street." He rebukes both of them, "You know how dangerous it is out there without a crew. I haven't had anyone watching my back in years. I'm flying solo because my fucking friends abandoned me."

Isaiah is taken aback by Tyler's indignant words. Jason is speechless and shakes his head in disbelief. And in the same instant, Tyler regrets all that he said. His remorse is evident by the way he hangs his head, but Isaiah doesn't let him off the hook.

"How you gonna talk to us like that? You self-righteous prick. Jason keeps us flush. His money lets us all live a comfortable life. Because of him, you work as you please, you paint as you please and you go bombing as you please. And from what I understand, you've been borrowing a little extra from him, haven't ya?"

Tyler shrinks away.

"Yeah, that's what I thought. And me—patrol the streets? You speak as if I'm some goddamn constable twirling a baton and working a beat. I'm a Magistrate Inquirer, motherfucker—*thee* Magistrate Inquirer, as far as you're concerned. I've stuck my neck out for you countless times, and I continue to keep an open ear and a watchful eye over us—which is imperative during these times. Now that's what we do for you. What exactly do you do for us?"

Tyler is silent. His face radiates regret. Still, Isaiah doesn't let him off the hook.

"I asked you a question."

Tyler delays answering. Isaiah waits.

"I did that one thing that one time."

Isaiah's body language shifts—he backs off, calms down.

"Yes. Yes, you did. And we're forever grateful for that. Just don't forget for one minute that we've been here for you too. The two of us may not write anymore, but we're still a crew."

"Yeah, I know," Tyler says, sincerely. "Look, I'm sorry. You know I didn't mean it. It's just that this is all very real and I need to clear my name and get back out there."

"You don't need to do shit right now. You sit tight for a while and I'll get you out of this. I can't do anything about the crown— nice work, by the way, and a real gutsy spot—but we'll crack the case, then the media will lose interest. You'll be back out there soon enough."

Jason chimes in. "Do what he says, Ty."

Tyler doesn't respond—just stares into his beer.

"You sure you ditched the can where nobody will find it?" Isaiah asks.

"Yeah, positive." Tyler pauses for a moment. "Any cameras?"

"Huh?"

"Was I caught on any security cameras?"

"No. You're fucking lucky. And I can't believe you didn't get the plate number. Just sit tight and let me do my thing. Two weeks, tops."

"Two weeks ... how can you be so sure?

"Because I know my shit."

Tyler bobs his head in contemplation. Jason and Isaiah trade glances.

"A'ight," Tyler concedes.

"Good. Now start us off," Isaiah demands.

Tyler rolls his eyes.

"Go on. You start. Just pretend like we're back at the lunch tables at LA High. It's good to remember those days."

"I know you mean well, Izzy, but it still doesn't feel right without her here."

"Well, we can't do anything about—"

Jason cuts in, "There is no I or me ..."

Isaiah continues, "There is only us and we ..."

Tyler reluctantly joins in, "That's how it is ...

Jason finishes, "And will always be."

Tyler sips at his beer then heads for the restroom.

As Tyler walks away, Jason turns to Isaiah.

"What's up with him lately? He doesn't come around as often and when he does, it's like he's detached from everything."

"I've noticed it, too."

"Things never were the same between us when I came back, but this ... this feels different—like something's really wrong with him."

"Yeah, I know. And he doesn't look well—like something's been eating at him."

"You don't think it's—"

"No, not that. We all got over that."

Jason nods, but his eyes squint with a hint of uncertainty.

"Izzy, I don't think he even knows about the march. A couple of years ago, he would've known about it before we did."

Isaiah puckers his lips and stares off.

"And listen, about this shit," Jason says, "you know he's not just going to sit around and wait. No matter what he says, he's going to get involved, and that'll make things worse."

"Yeah ... you're right." Isaiah exhales in frustration. "Alright. Okay. I'll take care of it."

The friends share a moment of comfortable silence.

"It's been a while since he's brought up Katy," Jason says, soberly.

"It's been a while for all of us."

"No matter how many women he cycles through, he'll never get over her."

Isaiah looks off to the side, remembering old times, before responding rhetorically. "Would you?"

Jason draws in a short breath and shakes his head with a somber look in his eyes.

Isaiah slides off the stool and Jason walks around the counter to say goodbye.

"Why's he been borrowing money from you anyway?" Isaiah asks.

"Dunno, man. I think he may've stopped racking."

"Ah. Makes sense. He's too old to be stealing shit. How deep is he?"

"Hundred stacks," Jason says, sheepishly.

Isaiah makes a wry face and scoffs. "Damn, that's some serious coin. He's been spending that on more than just paint."

Jason shrugs. "Maybe so."

Isaiah and Jason clasp hands and bring each other in for a one-armed hug. While embracing they each whisper, "VoHé."

Tyler returns from the restroom and reprises the role of sulking patron on barstool. It takes much too long for him to realize that Isaiah is no longer at the bar. He sits and he drinks and he thinks.

I can't stop, man. I just can't. I gotta keep getting up. I'll go crazy if I don't keep getting up. I gotta figure this out. All those years building a rep ... I gotta clear my name ... clear SOBR's name. The pigs don't want the truth, they just wanna pin this on someone ... on me. This is too big. It's out of Isaiah's control. Besides, it's just a mystery ... a riddle ... and it can be solved like all other riddles.

Alright, how do I do this? Where do I start?

The crime scene. Of course. Tomorrow I'll go back to the alley and look around.

The tavern has grown crowded. Standing room only.

Faye enters the bar with a man. Tyler sees her and quickly looks away. He spies on her out of the corner of his eye. She flirts with the gentleman suitor and when she catches Tyler watching her, his eyes conspicuously awry, she exaggerates her flirtation—bigger laughs, playful touching.

The fuck is she trying to do? Make me jealous?

Fed up with watching Faye philander, Tyler exits the tavern.

At home, Tyler proceeds straight to his bedroom, ignoring his housemates and their friends who are assembled in the living room. The audience sits on the floor, like pupils gathered around a teacher, as the stern one speaks calmly yet passionately in the middle of a lesson.

"The standard of living that Americans have come to enjoy—Convenience and Choice and all the things that follow with it—this way of life—is it a moral one? Is it the standard to which all other nations should strive to achieve? Before we answer that, we must first look at some of the effects of this way of life. So, what unavoidably ensues with a lifestyle of Convenience and Choice? There are a number of consequences, of course, but I want to look at the most obvious among them—Waste.

"Americans have a voracious appetite for all things. To maintain their way of life, they must constantly consume the things made available to them. Their systems are set up not only to provide them with all the things their hearts desire, but also new models of those things on a regular basis. Thus, things become unwanted and discarded not because they cease to function, but simply because there are new versions of the things.

"And there are also things that are intentionally designed to be used for a short period of time and then thrown away—plastic utensils, condoms and candy wrappers; coffee cups and lids and stirrers; tubes of hair, skin and dental products; lighters, pens and credit cards… you get the idea, and I'll spare you the lecture on the immorality of Planned Obsolescence.

"The waste generated by this way of life is astonishing.

"Not only are the things themselves abandoned, but also the time, money and energy it took to acquire the things. So, when you see landfills overflowing with discarded things and the boxes, bags and plastics used to label, transport and market those things, know that it is not only garbage that lives in the dumps, but also a significant portion of the American life.

"And where do the things come from? Often not from America, but from other nations that are stuck in an economic cycle of having to manufacture the things. Why are the things largely affordable? Because the people of these other nations labor cheaply and, yes, even slave, to supply the Convenience and Choice that Americans have become accustomed to.

"Now I ask you, should all other nations aspire to this way of life?

"If you have any doubt, ask yourself this: Who would make the things for all of them? And if all nations are somehow able to achieve this way of life, does Earth possess the resources to support the demand for all the things? Could it manage the resulting waste? I think not. No, if all nations were to live like Americans, the world would experience a crisis of sustainability beyond all measure.

"My point is this—if a particular way of life is not sustainable if it were to be adopted on a global basis, then that way of life is fundamentally immoral."

Eyes light up with epiphany.

Ping.

Tyler's god machine calls out and lights up on his nightstand.

> Dizzy Izzy
> -I know ur thinking about
> figuring this out on your own. So
> I'll make you a deal… interested?
>
> -Depends
> -U know what, forget it
>
> -Ok ok
> -I'm interested
> -There are certain people I go
> to for info in situations like this.
> Sometimes they know shit,
> sometimes they don't
>
> -Snitches?
> -No. Just people I know… and
> don't ever use that word again
> -I don't have time to see them all,
> so I'll send u to see some of
> them and gather intel
>
> -Is that even allowed?
> -I think u will agree that we
> stopped playing by the rules a
> long time ago
>
> -Right
> -Okay, I'm in
> -Good. I'll text u an address
> tomorrow. Stay at home and
> keep ur phone near
> -And DO NOT go back to the
> piece. Cameras r there now
>
> -Wasn't planning to
> -Yeah, whatever

Tyler turns off his bedside lamp and tries to fall asleep.

The Second Hymn.

The choir finishes the first hymn and the members reposition themselves on the stage. Tyler hardly notices the shift as he selects a seat among the pews. As soon as his body comes to rest in the notch of the wooden bench, his mind trips and stumbles down the precipice of consciousness, garnering speed with each passing second as it descends into the gorge of hypnotic abstraction. The chorus begins the second hymn—a vociferous psalm from behind those hideous masks.

> Holy, Holy, Holy! Lord God Aesymnetes!
> Early in the morning, VoHé our voices ring;
> Holy, Holy, Holy! Thunderous and Mighty!
> Twice-born, thigh-born, son of Semele.
>
> Holy, Holy, Holy! All the satyrs love Thee,
> Chasing 'round the forest nymphs, dancing the sikinnis;
> Maenads and bacchants falling down before Thee,
> Which always was and forever shall be.
>
> Holy, Holy, Holy! Though chaos follows Thee,
> Without your 'chanted wine, Thy glory we ne'er do see;
> Our heads crowned with ivy, we rave in ecstasy,
> In wine we find madness and epiphany.
>
> Holy, Holy, Holy! Lord God Aesymnetes!
> All Thy beasts shall praise Thy name, from here and there to Crete;
> Holy, Holy, Holy! Thunderous and Mighty!
> Twice-born, thigh-born, son of Semele.

7

Tyler doesn't sleep, at least not soundly. All night he's in that restless state of excitement and anxiety that prevents one from entering slow-wave sleep, that deep sleep that affords the brain the opportunity to recover from stress, consolidate memories and solve problems—a prerequisite to the stage of slumber referred to as REM. Tyler nods off and wakes up. Nods off and wakes up. Nods off and wakes up. Each time he wakes he's unable to determine how long he's been asleep—has it been two minutes, or two hours?

Tyler lies flat on his back, his eyes wide open as the color beyond his bedroom window transitions from smoky gray to powder blue.

Has Isaiah texted yet?

He checks his phone. Nothing. He flips over onto his stomach, nods off and wakes up. He checks his phone. Nothing. He stirs and reluctantly gets out of bed. He checks his phone. Nothing. He takes a shower. He checks his phone. Nothing. He shaves. He checks his phone. Nothing. He brushes and flosses his teeth. He checks his phone. Nothing. He prepares breakfast and sips coffee. He checks his phone. Nothing. He cleans the dishes. He checks his phone. Nothing. He sits on the sofa in the living room and watches television. He checks his phone. Nothing.

Sandra Alvarez interrupts the mindless Saturday morning programming with a news bulletin:

GOOD MORNING, SOUTHLANDERS. Breaking news this morning as authorities announce that a reward has been offered for any information leading to the arrest of the graffiti vandal known as SOBR. Authorities say that any person who provides information that is instrumental in assisting them with the apprehension and questioning of the elusive vandal will be entitled to claim a reward in an amount up to ten thousand dollars. This announcement comes on the heels of the discovery of a dead man behind a CVS in South Central LA early Friday morning. Authorities still have not released the identity of the deceased, or whether they believe that the mysterious vandal is a suspect in the murder. Members of the public are encouraged to report any information through a dedicated tip hotline. Please call the number provided on the screen below. And now back to regularly scheduled programming.

Yeah, twenty-five hundred. It's in the muni code.

Ten thousand! What the fuck?

Goddammit.

Tyler reaches for his god machine to check in with Isaiah and figure out what the fuck is going on.

Dizzy Izzy
-What the fuck is going on?
-Why's the reward so high?

-I know. It caught me by surprise
too
-Things are moving quickly on
this one. Just chill and stick to
the plan
                    -What plan? You haven't sentme
                                         anything yet
-Soon. Chill the fuck out
-And don't do anything stupid

But Tyler can't chill the fuck out.
He sets out to do something stupid.

Arms crossed, Tyler leans against a gray awning post on the
platform of the Exposition Line, waiting for the eastbound train.
The hood of his sweatshirt is drawn over a black-on-black Los
Angeles Rams ballcap, which sits low on his brow, the bill nearly
resting on the top of his sunglasses. The awning post is directly in
front of a staircase that accesses the raised platform and Tyler takes
in the tableau of LA life as the commuters come and go: A woman
bending over a stroller to entertain her baby. An elderly man and
his husband walking hand-in-hand. Two teenagers canoodling on
one of the benches. A man enjoying what must be one of the few
pleasures available to him—a beverage sheathed in a brown paper
bag. A woman and her two lovers walking arm-in-arm. A group of
teenage skaters indiscreetly passing around a joint. A large woman
in a motorized wheelchair humming across the platform. A cyclist
squirting water into his mouth from a plastic water bottle.
    An automated notice announces the imminent arrival of the
eastbound train and reminds commuters to remain behind the yellow
line. Tyler shoves his hands in the pockets of his hoodie and uncaps
a small Molotow marker with his right hand.
    The train comes to a full stop and the doors of the railcars open.
A few commuters trickle out of the cars and those waiting on the
platform begin to enter. Tyler turns and faces the post with his body
close to it. He removes his hands from his pockets and conceals
the Molotow in the tuck of his palm. His actions are quick and
deliberate. He pumps the marker to release liquid paint to the felt tip.
When the felt is good and soaked, he draws an upside down crown

on the gray post. His hands retract to his pockets and he boards the nearest railcar just as the doors begin to close.

Tyler plops down on one of the benches situated against the wall of the railcar. He looks side-to-side from under the protection of his sunglasses to see if anyone stares him down as if to say "yeah, I saw what you did." But nobody looks at him. Nobody looks at anyone. All heads are lowered in prayer to their personal god machines. Their thumbs and index fingers engaged in an orgy of sacred dance and worship. Their eyes darting in and out of focus as they study blogs and social media feeds like holy scrolls. This tragic scene— these people not bothering to be present, to be aware, content with moving through life with their heads bowed.

The train approaches the next station. Tyler stands near the door of the railcar, but not directly in front of it. He wants to be the last one to exit the car and doesn't want anyone else to be obstructed from quick egress. His left hand grips a chrome railing above his head and his right hand clutches the small weapon of mass defacement in his pocket. As the train decelerates, he uncaps the Molotow marker. The train stops and the doors open. He scans the car to see if anyone is making their way to exit. Nope, nobody. He turns his back to the cabin of the railcar and scribbles an upside down crown on the laminated wall before hopping off the train. The doors close behind him and the bored faces of the communers are whisked away. Nobody saw him—or everybody saw him, but nobody gives a fuck. Either way is fine with Tyler.

Tyler walks to the awning post closest to the platform staircase and leans against it with crossed arms, patiently waiting to repeat the offense.

He goes about this for over an hour, platform to platform, railcar to railcar, tag after tag. Sometimes he leaves a rail station to tag the toppled crown on the gray masts of the traffic signals, just above the pedestrian push-button at all four corners of an intersection. He skips only the stations near the local university where the undergraduate brats, many of whom hail from the more wholesome areas of the country—er, kingdom—are naïve enough to cause a scene. He places upside down crowns in prominent locations all along a well-travelled path, but he never signs his name. Public awareness of that pseudonym is too high right now and the purpose of this exercise is to simply sow dissent and kill time until Isaiah contacts him—

Ping.

—which occurs imminently.

                    Dizzy Izzy
    -Alright u need to go see my
    boy Shawn and his momma in
    Inglewood
                              -Address?
    -Yeah, I know u need the
    address. U need to fucking chill
    out
    -1121 82nd pl
                    -What am I supposed to do?
    -They have some info but don't
    wanna tell me over the phone.
    Can't trust the phones these
    days.
    -They're expecting u. Just listen
    to them and be on ur best
    behavior

Tyler summons a car.

8

The chauffer drops Tyler off in front of a quaint house on a quiet tree-lined street. Standing curbside, the house appears well-kept. The yellow paint is bright and clean. The front windows sparkle and the white trim beams with a lustrous sheen. The lawn and the shrubs along the house are impeccably manicured. Two sculpted Cypress trees flank an arched entranceway that leads to the front porch. A silver Cadillac CTS sedan glistens in the driveway. And it's not just this house that's in good external repair—all of the houses on the street are in the same pleasant condition. The neighborhood is quite picturesque and not at all consistent with one's preconceived perception of Inglewood.

Tyler walks up a cement path that divides the front lawn in half. The arched entranceway is guarded by a steel screen door and outfitted with a doorbell and intercom system that peeks out from behind one of the Cypress trees. Above the intercom speaker is a sign fashioned from the torn flap of a cardboard beer box. In black ink from the thick tip of a Sharpie, hasty handwriting spells out: No Cell Phones. No Exceptions.

Tyler pushes the button and the intercom comes alive.

"Yeah, what?" says a deep voice.

"Uh, hi. This is Tyler. I think you're expecting me."

"Hold up."

The voice returns.

"Who sent you?"

"Isaiah."

"Who?"

Uncertain of the proper etiquette and starting to sweat a bit, Tyler glances over his shoulder, crouches close to the speaker and whispers, "Magistrate Carver."

"Speak up, muhfuckah."

"Uh, Magistrate Carver sent me."

"Hold up."

The voice returns.

"A'ight, you good."

There's a sudden buzzing followed by the audible release of a locking mechanism in the screen door, like being let in to a pawn shop past curfew hours.

Tyler opens the portcullis and enters the porch with a hint of trepidation. The front door to the house is ajar and a man greets him.

"I'm Shawn. C'mon in." The deep voice is friendly, but oddly disproportionate to the size of the man.

Tyler steps through the threshold, which leads directly into an ordinary living room—sofa, couple of recliners, fireplace with family photos on the mantel, thin flat screen TV, gaming consoles—all of the furnishings are new and high quality.

"Have a seat, don't be shy. Momma will be out soon."

Tyler sits down on the sofa and takes off his sunglasses. From this angle he can see into the hallway and the dining room, each of which is filled with rows upon rows of cardboard banker boxes, stacked at least five high. The stacks are neat and orderly, a printed list of contents affixed on the side of each box. Tyler knits his brow and is overcome with flashbacks of his former office job.

"First things first, Tyler. Cell phone."

"What?"

"Cell phone."

Tyler stares blankly.

"You did see the sign outside, did you not?"

"Uh, yeah."

"A'ight, then. Cell phone. Do you have one on you?"

"Yes."

"Hand it over."

Tyler apprehensively does as instructed.

"And you saw the sign said 'no exceptions,' right?"

"Yes, but I figured that—"

"You figured wrong."

Shawn drops the phone to the hardwood floor and stomps on it with the thick heel of a Timberland boot until the device is smashed to bits, all while Tyler protests in a stammering flurry of "dude" and "stop" and "what the fuck!"

Shawn finally relents. He looks Tyler directly in the eyes as he kneels down, flips the phone over, what's left of it, and starts stomping again.

After Shawn finishes thoroughly destroying the phone, he says, with resolution, "No. Exceptions."

"But ... but I'm here on *official* business."

"Show me your badge."

Tyler doesn't respond. He sulks and looks away.

"That's what I thought. You're as official as fuck, muhfuckah. And besides, the rule also applies to the officials. You broke the rule and this is what happens."

Before Tyler could utter another word of protest, Momma cuts in as she makes her way down the hallway and into the living room.

"Sorry about that, hunnie. Can't be too careful these days." She hands Shawn a plastic Ziploc bag as she walks by. She's a curvy woman of a certain age who takes pride in her appearance—nails done, hair done, everything did.

Shawn gathers the shattered pieces of Tyler's god machine, places them in the bag, zips it shut and tosses it on the coffee table in front of Tyler. Tyler stares at it with dull eyes and a clenched jaw while Momma takes a seat in one of the leather recliners.

"Well now, I suppose we have your attention and I can see that you're processing things, hunnie, so I'll do the talking for now. Before we get down to"—she leans in and says "official" with a wink—"business, I want to let you know a little bit about us. I think that's only fair since Officer Carver told us so much about you before your arrival." Momma pauses to gather her thoughts before continuing, "To put it frankly, hunnie, we're thieves. The good kind, mind you, and I think you'll agree. You see these boxes all around here—wonder what they are? Just nod your head, hunnie."

Tyler nods in the affirmative.

"These boxes contain the tax filings of many good people around the hood and the greater Los Angeles area. You see, Shawn and I are... well, accountants, of a sort. For a fair percentage, we help the people take back what they deserve, and"—Momma chuckles—"oh, maybe a little more, from His Majesty's Internal Revenue Service. Some of our clients are just in it for the money, but many of them are Insurrectionists—much like you are, as I've been led to believe.

Tyler's unclenches his jaw.

"You doing okay there, hunnie? You look pale. Or perhaps that's just your natural complexion." She lets out a self-satisfied cackle.

"Don't look so dumbfounded, muhfuckah. Let me guess—you come to a Black man's house in Inglewood, you see the new Caddy in the driveway and the nice things up in here, so you assumed we sell drugs—am I right?"

"Uh—"

"You don't have to answer that, hunnie. He's just being dramatic."

"Thank you," Tyler says, relieved.

Shawn puckers his lips, narrows his eyes, and folds his arms in disdain. Momma goes on.

"Our Insurrectionist clients have talents of their own and we all operate, more or less, as a collective to undermine the King. I understand from Officer Carver that you might be interested in helping us. Is that right?"

"Uh, well ... maybe ... I don't know."

"That doesn't sound promising," Shawn says. "Momma, you told him too much. This boy's gotta go."

Tyler quickly squeaks out a question, "What about audits?"

"Questions already? That's good," Momma says in delighted fashion. She looks to Shawn in that condescending I-told-you-so sort of way, and then continues.

"As long as my name and signature appear on the tax returns when they're filed, our clients don't get audited. Well, not so much anymore. We have certain … arrangements. Our clients are not just gangsters and hoodrats, as you may be inclined to assume. They're working people with collars white and blue—plumbers, electricians, landscapers, doctors, lawyers, teachers, you name it. And some of them work"—Momma leans in—"*internally*, you understand?"

Tyler nods in the affirmative.

"Oh, every now and again there's an eager upstart brat who tries to audit some of our clients and we deal with the little shit appropriately—"

"Yeah, we got an audit protection plan," Shawn interrupts, casually lifting his shirt to reveal the grip of a Glock poking out above his waistband.

"Hush now, son."

"Sorry, momma."

"Hunnie, time is limited and I think you understand the nature of what's going on here. I have one question for you. Where do you worship?" Momma asks Tyler.

"Uh, well, I try to go to the late services at The Eternal Church of the Bakkheia."

"Mmm, yes, I know it. I've heard good things. I should stop by sometime to observe and offer libation. We attend The Rising Sun of Apollo up on Crenshaw. Listen, Tyler, I'm a good judge of character and I like your vibe. I think our ethos, while probably not identical, is certainly simpatico. Tax season approaches and we're anticipating an increase in volume. We need help processing the paperw—"

"If there even is a tax season this year," Shawn interrupts.

"Shawn! Hush! I'm sure Tyler knows all about that already." Momma continues, "Anyway, hunnie, Office Carver told us about your political persuasions and your background in accounting—a couple of seasons at H&R Block is good enough for us. He thought you might be interested in helping us steal from the King. He vouched for you, hunnie. You know what that means, right?"

Tyler nods in the affirmative.

"So what do you say—want to join us and be a regular Robin Hood? We'll give you a fair vig, details to be worked out some other ti—"

"Nuh-uh, no fuckin' way!" Shawn interjects. "Momma, he can help us out, but he ain't no Robin Hood. That would make us his band of Merry Moors—no way!" With his finger pointed at Tyler, he commands, "Muhfuckah, you're only robbin' *for* the hood, got it?"

"Hush, son! He hasn't even answered, yet. Let the man think."

"Sorry, momma." Then to Tyler, "Go on. Think, muhfuckah."

Tyler looks intrigued, like he's about to agree. But he retreats into himself for a split-second—flashes of pigtails and jagged black teeth, observable only by his subconscious, remind him that any time spent away from painting and catching tags is time wasted.

"Thanks for the offer, but that life's not for me anymore."

Momma and Shawn trade curious glances.

Shawn says, "What's that mean muh—"

"Shawn, for the last time—hush! And arrange for a car to pick up our guest. His time here is near its end."

Shawn quickly retrieves his god machine and bids for a car, glad to soon be rid of the guest.

"Okay, hunnie, but know that it's an open offer. If you change your mind, just give us a call. In the meantime, you can tell Officer Carver that the body traveled from beyond the dusk."

"From beyond the dusk?"

"Mm-hmm."

"What does that mean?"

"It's not for me to say, but you're a clever boy and I'm sure you'll figure it out. You just be sure to relay the message.

Well, this has been a pleasant visit and I do believe we are well-met. Let it be the will of Apollo that our paths cross again. Shawn will walk you out now."

Momma and Tyler stand up. Momma leaves the living room as Tyler says, "Likewise, it was nice to meet you, Ms.—"

"You can just call me 'Momma,' hunnie," she says over her shoulder as she disappears into the hallway.

Shawn and Tyler stand in the enclosed porch until the car arrives. Tyler holds the Ziploc bag with his broken spirit in it.

"She told you to call her 'Momma.' That means she likes you.

And I guess that means I have to, too. Don't mean I want you coming 'round here very often though."

"Uh, thanks?"

"A'ight then. Yo, you need some weed before you go?"

Tyler cocks his head. "I thought you said you don't sell drugs."

"I ain't never said that. You need to work on your listening skills. Besides, we don't sell drugs—we *also* sell drugs. There's a difference. We're big-time tax, small-time weed. So, what you need?"

"Sure, I'll take a dime bag."

Shawn snickers.

"You can just say 'dime.' Here... take this." Shawn pulls a baggy of weed and a one-hitter cigarette pipe from his shirt pocket and hands them to Tyler. "It's a homegrown strain. On the house."

"Cool, thanks."

"Careful—it'll get you fucked up."

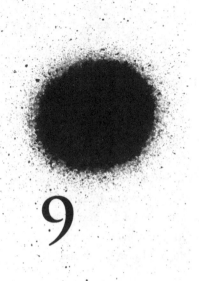

9

The driver lets Tyler out in a parking lot adjacent to the nearest rail station as instructed.

Tyler slides out of the car and asks, "Hey, you got a light?"

"Yeah, sure. Here you go."

"Can I buy it off you?"

The driver flashes a look of annoyance and says, "Nah, dude, just keep it."

"Thanks, man."

Tyler shuts the door and the car rolls away.

Tyler walks toward the platform and spots a trash can. A twinge of anger sparks behind his eyes as he discards the Ziploc bag containing his shattered digital deity. He lets out a sigh then scans his TAP card and hops up the stairs of the westbound platform.

Sunglasses on, hat low, hood up—Tyler leans against a post, arms folded, again soaking in the beauty of the urban ebb and flow. He's ready to repeat the inverted crown assault on all trains and platforms on the way to the opening night of Mollusk's long-awaited exhibition. He lets his eyes wander about the platform until he spots a curious marking at the far end of the terrace.

No way.

He walks toward it.

It can't be.

The marking comes into focus—the image of an upside down crown has been scratched in the fiberglass window of the rail line map. The corner of Tyler's mouth twitches and cascades into a full grin.

An automated voice announces the arrival of a train over the loudspeaker. Tyler collects himself, scribbles on the post nearest to him and then slips into the closest railcar. The doors shut and another upside down crown slides into view on one of the windows—the letters FTK appearing on the other window—not his ink and not his style.

Tyler is invigorated. His energy levels spike so much so that his spirit cannot contain the dynamism. His essence releases a minute measure of the amassing pressure in a sort of kinetic pulse that propels a disc of unseen energy from the epicenter of his being. The energy ripples out into the cabin of the railcar like a water ring traveling away from a droplet.

If any of the passengers sense the effect of the energy passing through them, it's in the form of horripilation—the phenomenon commonly referred to as goose bumps. Some contend that the occurrence of goose bumps is vestigial, that ever since humans lost their fur, leaving nothing left to stand on end, it no longer serves a practical purpose. That it has no function in this evolutionary phase of the human system. But just because fur has disappeared from the human epidermis does not mean that the nervous system has ceased to signal meaningful events that would otherwise go unperceived by the Self. Indeed, the human mind and body are rife with mysterious function and ceremony that people ignore or fail to thoroughly explore. Maybe such indifference is due to short attention spans spawned by digital distraction or rampant consumerism; or maybe it's due to career obsession, or misinformation that follows with religion; or maybe it simply has always been. Whatever the reason, people routinely fail to heed the innate messages and warnings that come from The Deep Within. Those messages and warnings that manifest in the form of the esoteric—such as intuition—or in the form of the physical—such as temporary pimply bumps that stand erect on the skin.

And so it is that none of the passengers grasp that the dermal phenomenon was interhuman in origin. Either they assume that a chill moved through the cabin, or they are so engrossed in digital veneration that they fail to notice the bristling of their own hide.

Save for one man. One man realizes.

Tyler removes his sunglasses and scans the cabin. Heads are bowed, fingers in adulation. He locks eyes with the man. The man's head is not bowed—he stares straight through Tyler with piercing brown eyes. His face is hard and worn, but it contains a reverence that could only have been formed from a lifetime of self-determination—it's the face of an OG, a *vato*, a man who has never bowed to anyone in his life, or who bows no longer.

The *vato* holds Tyler's gaze in a way that communicates awareness and discernment. He shifts his eyes in the direction of the crown scrawled on the window and then nods his head in a quick upward motion. Although Tyler is not the author of this particular work, he has no doubt that it exists because of him, so he responds with a single downward nod. The *vato* strokes his salt-and-pepper mustache, the size of which would make Zapata proud.

The *vato* stands as the train slows to a stop. He runs his hands down the front of his plaid Pendleton shirt to smooth out the wrinkles. Tyler steps back and braces himself for conflict. The *vato* smirks and doffs the wide brim of his fedora as a sign of approval and valediction before exiting the train.

The exchange, though seemingly inconsequential, is significant to Tyler. It validates the medium of his art. It confirms that his message resonates with people.

These days the working people live hard lives—days filled with exertion and uncertainty and little reward. The struggle, as they say, is real. It seems as if opportunity for those who are not born into privilege is limited to low-skilled, low-paying, hard-labor jobs. And sure, someone has got to do those jobs. But it's becoming shamefully easy to predict who that certain someone will be. Of course, some lucky few will break through, pulling themselves up by their bootstraps. But the notion of The American Dream, open and available to everyone who seeks it, has all but faded away. And what remains may as well be a rigged national lottery. The working people have caught on—and they are not happy.

So, the waters of discontent have risen to a meniscus resting delicately above the levee of a vast lake. As a single droplet can rupture the surface tension and initiate a flood, so too can graffiti spur insurgency.

This is how the revolution begins—with Molotows, not Molotovs.

Don't everybody like the smell of gasoline?

10

Tyler exits the train at La Cienega and Jefferson. He bounds
down the platform stairs and meanders down the busy thoroughfare,
stopping every so often to scribble an inverted crown. He comes
across a chain link fence that separates the street from the banks
of a small watershed known as Ballona Creek. He ducks under a
clipped section of the fence and ambles along the dirt embankment.
A hamlet of makeshift dwellings lines the other side of the creek—a
dismal carnival of vibrantly colored umbrellas and tarps and
shopping carts. A smoldering haze wafts up from the center of the
encampment like some pitiful smoke signal, and the surrounding
area smells of burning Styrofoam and baked beans. The small
fire provides a means of cooking and temporary warmth for the
inhabitants, but the fumes beckon Death to their location like a
perilous GPS system.

Tyler comes to an area shaded by a short palm tree and sits on
an overturned wooden crate. He pulls out the baggy of weed and
packs a small hit in the thin cigarette-like pipe. He strikes the wheel
of the lighter with his thumb and the gift of Prometheus appears
in the palm of his hand. He brings the flame to the tip of the pipe

and takes a hit to the dome, holding the smoke in his lungs before letting it out slow. Tiny THC soldiers deployed from the cerebellum march on Fort Limbs, conquering flesh and leaving the battlefield euphoric and numb. HQ radios for reinforcements and once more Tyler deploys the troops who forge into battle with arrogant gusto, their eyes having seen the glory of the coming of the Lord and that place where the grapes of wrath are stored. Truth marches on. Glory fucking halleluiah.

Tyler blows the ash out from the pipe and pockets the contraband. He shuts his eyes and leans back against the palm tree with a stupid grin on his face.

A wanderer strolls along the creek near Tyler, stopping here and there to examine bits of potential treasure hiding in the dirt and crabgrass. The stranger is old and mangy. Eyes cloudy with cataracts. The kind of beggar that reminds you that you should donate money to a shelter, but the kind you never stop to help. The kind you ignore as you walk by. The kind you would never let into your home. The kind whose existence is proof that we are not actually kind.

The wanderer slinks toward Tyler and takes a seat on the ground a few feet away from him. Tyler glances at the wanderer out of the corner of his faded eyes—his nose twitches at the stench.

Tyler hears the wanderer start to speak, as if to nobody in particular.

"Shit's fucked up, man. Shit's real fucked up."

Tyler doesn't acknowledge him. The wanderer becomes distracted by something that scurries by and disappears into the earth. He giggles and mutters something to himself before rambling on.

"Been out here seeing it all. Seeing it all happen for years. It doesn't matter to me. None of it can touch me. I already have nothing. But they're comin'. They've been comin'. Year after year. Comin' to take for themselves. Thing is, there's nothin' left to take. So what's next?"

They sit there—species from different walks of life united only by the simple pleasure of a gentle breeze.

Tyler responds without looking at the wanderer, "Dunno. I tune most of it out. I have to—it's too soul-crushing otherwise."

The wanderer looks over at Tyler with surprise. "Oh, so you *can* hear me. Most people just ignore me and leave. But I had a feeling about you—you're one of the good ones."

"Nah." Tyler shakes his head. "I don't think so."

"We're organizing though. Yes sir, getting organized. It'll be a beautiful thing when it happens—leveling the playing field and all that. 'Fraid I'll miss it though. I've lived many lives and I think this one is just about done. Yes, I'm a clear vessel operating on frequency nine."

Tyler furrows his brow and dismisses the wanderer's incomprehensible rambling.

"I'll return, of course. You won't, though. You are diverged, man—your vessel's not clear and you've forgotten your frequency, just like the rest of you. Despicable."

The wanderer jerks his head up and stares directly into the sun. Then, without saying a word, he hops up and pitter-patters along the embankment, leaving tiny tracks in the dirt path.

Tyler closes his eyes, intent on savoring what's left of his body buzz—the footsteps of those invisible soldiers marching in formation on newly occupied territory, singing songs of victory—before heading to the gallery.

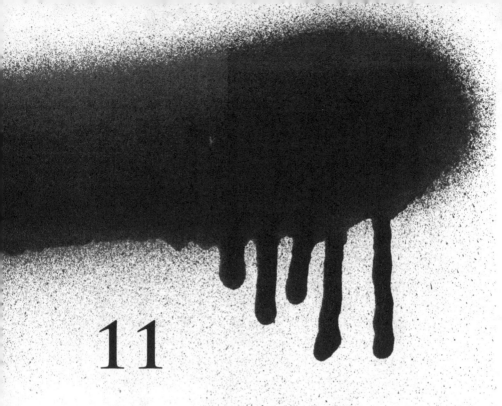

11

Devereaux Fine Arts is located in a non-descript brick building situated in the back of an industrial park on the eastside of Culver City. It's identified only by a wrought iron sign containing the letters DFA bolted in the masonry to the left of the entrance.

Tyler hands the doorman his driver's license. While shifting it back-and-forth in one hand, the doorman flashes an ultraviolet light on the card to authenticate the holograms embedded in the laminate. The doorman hands the card back to Tyler along with two drink tickets for the host bar inside.

The entrance leads into an enormous, multilevel space with an asymmetrical floorplan. The ground is a polished gray concrete. Metallic conduit and ventilation ducts run along the exposed fifty-foot ceiling and down the aged brickwork. The featured artwork hangs against crisp white drywall sporadically placed around the bottom level of the sprawling space. Some works hang in plain view and some are tucked away in alcoves. In the center of the room, a wide staircase leads to an upper level that protrudes over the back quarter of the space like a vast veranda. This upper floor hosts the DJ, the host bar and, according to Faye, a showing of Tyler's paintings—a series of irreverent triptychs inspired by Hieronymus Bosch—oil on wood panel, with Tyler's real name signed in the bottom-right corner.

As Tyler walks into the room, a second attendant hands him a show card—an introduction to the exhibition written by the featured artist, printed on glossy cardstock.

The room is in a constant flux. Waiters circle the room carrying trays of *hors d'oeuvres* while the DJ spins an assortment of trip hop, alt-R&B and neo soul. A group of girls take a selfie in front of one of the hanging works to upload it to their whatever-account. As Tyler skims the crowd, the shifting throng opens to reveal the honoree standing at the mouth of the stairway.

Andrew Mollusk is a relic of the once burgeoning Los Angeles punk scene. After achieving moderate success, his band split up and he spent the following few years tramping around the kingdom—or the country, as it was then-called—on the rails as a vagabond. The years on the road transformed him—he quit drinking, lost his hot temper and embraced an ascetic lifestyle. When he settled back in town, he sold nearly all of his possessions, including the majority of his music equipment and memorabilia, and he adopted the wardrobe of a friar, dressing almost exclusively in earthy tones of frocks and chiton. He let his hair and beard grow long, giving him that look of distinguished disarray—like a fusion of Francis of Assisi and Rick Rubin.

A pair of dirty Chuck Taylor High Tops peeks out from under Andrew's clerical garb. He's surrounded by sycophants who are praising his work and indulging his anecdotes. They gather around him in a semi-circle and the whole scene makes Andrew appear as some punk rock ecclesiast whose disciples are eagerly waiting for him to turn water into wine, praise Bacchus.

Andrew spots Tyler and he rocks his head to one side as if to say, "take a look around and we'll catch up soon." Tyler nods back and reviews the show card as he makes his way to the first painting.

[Front]
You see an image of the *chef d'oeuvre* of the exhibition.

With special thanks to Lesley Devereux and Tyler K.

Represented by Devereux Fine Arts
Culver City, California | Paris, France

Special thanks? Wow! What'd I do to deserve the honor?

[Back]
EVIL EMPIRE AND THE MONSTERS OF FUTURE LORE

Thank you for coming tonight. Allow me to set the stage of this exhibition: Millennia have passed since The Great Collapse, the inevitable consequence of ignoring all major economic and environmental crises that threaten humanity today. Digital technology was wiped out during the Nu-Dark Age that followed The Great Collapse. Nearly all evidence of our society—electronic and tech dependent, such as it is—disappeared into the ether. Our literature, our music, our films, our pictures, our medical records, our podcasts, our fucking tweets—virtually all evidence of our society was forever lost. And over time, the paper records, those last annals of our existence, decomposed into oblivion. However, as humans evolved and adapted to their decaying habitat, stories of the Evil Empire—the loathed stewards of The Great Collapse—were passed down through the generations. Much like the oral tradition of our ancestors, as stories are told and retold, forgotten and rediscovered, interpreted and misunderstood, they morph and they blend—they become distorted tales with hints of truth. Perhaps some of the tales evolved innocently and organically over the millennia, or perhaps some were devised by a cult of subversive historians as admonitory fairy tales for children and sardonic parables for adults. In any event, the accounts of our existence are nothing more than fable and folklore—facts woven with fiction—to the far-future humans (if that's what we/they still call ourselves/themselves). This series is a written and illustrated depiction of the myths and cautionary tales belonging to a distant humanity—The People of the Sun. This is an envisagement of our wretched legacy.

Mother. Fucker.

Tyler paces the floor of the gallery in a state of smoldering detachment—the net result of simultaneously processing equal rations of rage and despair. His eyes are glazed, limbs numb, stomach knotted, as he views many of the paintings and reads the corresponding plaques.

You see two ancient, mythical-looking dwarves. One sits on a tree stump and the other stands just behind the seated dwarf's right shoulder. Both have long, gray hair and thick beards. The standing dwarf wears a stereotypical Viking helmet and his right hand rests on the handle of a shovel in upright position. The seated dwarf wears a white breastplate decorated with a red Cross of Lorraine embroidered at an angle that's slightly askew. Their clothes are embellished with an ornate red and blue zigzag pattern. You look into their eyes, black and beady, and you shudder as their expressions convey insatiable desire. Silhouettes of hydraulic fracturing drills and oil rigs emerge from the background. You look at the bottom of the painting and see that the blade of the shovel and the dwarves' tall leather boots rest upon a pile of lifeless fish and wildlife all drenched in oil.

The Chevrexx $10,000
Mixed media on panel, 24" x 24"   Sold

The People of the Sun will recall the cautionary tale of the tribe known as The Chevrexx. Their lives were dedicated to extracting materials from deep in the soil and the oceans. The Chevrexx began as a modest people with good intentions, possessing only rudimentary methods and tools to carry out their trade. As time went on, their numbers grew in population and in wealth, and their tools became more sophisticated and efficient. Their machines could extract great volumes from the earth, but these same tools that could produce maximum yield would also give way to maximum catastrophe. Despite numerous disasters wreaking havoc upon the environment, killing untold numbers of fish and wildlife, and polluting the water table, the people did not rise against the Chevrexx. No, the people were dependent on The Chevrexx, and their influence spread across the globe like a virus. The people cut deals with The Chevrexx and legislated lenient laws for them to follow. Eventually, The Chevrexx stole from the land as their hearts desired to the great benefit of their personal gain. But the Chevrexx delved too greedily and too deep— they unleashed shadow and fire. The Earth succumbed to tremors and quakes. The land spilled in on itself without warning, leaving holes that could not be filled. Lakes disappeared overnight. And flame spewed from the ground.

You see two people, curiously dressed, standing and facing each other on a cracked desert basin. Their body language is that of inflated indignation and stubbornness. On the left is a muscular young man. He is scarcely clothed, wearing only tall combat boots, shiny gold dolphin shorts, a silk ascot around his bare torso, and an over-sized felt top hat. He has a Wall Street Journal-branded fanny pack slung around one hip and a military belt with a leather-bound canteen attached to it on the other hip. Despite the odd costume, you would swear that this man's closet is filled with clothes from Lacoste and Brooks Brothers, and that his name is something like Patrick or Gordon, or Randolph or Mortimer. On the right is a fit young woman. And she, too, is meagerly clad. She wears furry pink boot coverings that almost reach her knees, skimpy bikini bottoms and a fluffy white bikini top that allows for maximum tanning exposure. A NASDAQ-branded fanny pack rests on her hip and a pair of ski goggles with mirrored lenses sits on her forehead. Faun ears and antlers are somehow fastened to her skull, and you could swear that her name is Blake or Leighton, or Serena or Blair. The quarreling pair's features are handsome and striking, their bronze skin glistens, but they reek of advantage and entitlement. In the background of the desert landscape, you see strange statues and vehicles, and cartoonish cacti of unnatural colors and shapes.

The Golden Sax $15,000
Mixed media on panel, 36" x 36"   Sold

The Golden Sax were a fraternal order of men and women born with a proclivity for generating money by complicated means investment. Their archenemy was a dim and fearful group called The Pheds, whose mandate was to observe the behavior of the Golden Sax and to hold them accountable for unfair practices. But, as tradition tells us, The Pheds were riddled with their own special stench of corruption, and the Sax were repeatedly able to persuade members of The Pheds to desert their own ranks and join with the greedy order. And all too often, the Sax were able to supplant a defected Phed with one of their own. Over just a few centuries, their stubborn pursuit of riches collapsed industries and ruined nations. As an illustration of their stubbornness, there's a tale of an encounter between two young Sax during a week-long statue-burning ritual in the desert: The two Sax independently set out on a walkabout. Each travelled along the same course, one going south and the other going north. Eventually they ran directly into each other on the desert playa. One Sax asked the other to move, but she refused. She demanded that the other Sax step aside so that she may pass by. As expected, he declined. There they stood arguing for hours, or even days, over who should move for whom.

So the Harvard-trained Sax puffed his chest full of pride.
"I never," he said, "let a bitch tell me to move to one side.
And I'll prove to you that I won't change my ways
If I have to stand here 'til the end of my days!"
"And I'll prove to YOU," shrieked the Wharton-trained Sax,
"That I can stand here 'til the earth below us cracks,
Or 'til the end of MY days! For I live by some rules
That I learned as a girl at my Ivy League school.
'Never budge!' Not for a friend, a colleague or a prick like you!
'Always win!' That's the important thing and my only worldview!"

You see that the setting of this painting is a vast forest, densely populated by pine trees. The silhouette of a refinery can be seen in the distance, the smokestacks producing the clouds you see in the sky. In the middle of the painting, you see a large but skinny and sickly-looking grizzly bear wearing an unbuttoned Dijon-yellow fatigue shirt over a white shirt collar and a seafoam green tie. The fatigue shirt is carelessly patched with the names and logos of several pesticide and pharmaceutical products, like sponsors asymmetrically stitched on a NASCAR racing jacket. You see that the bear's eyes are wild and bloodshot, housed in dark circles like the eyes of a tweaker at the peak of a methamphetamine high, or those of a paranoid schizophrenic bound in a straitjacket and bouncing off the padded walls of a round room. The bear flashes a maniacal smile as he discharges a flamethrower at a beehive that hangs in a pine tree in the foreground. The hive is half scorched, and tiny winged flares try to fly away while the seared carcasses of unlucky bees fall to the ground. Your eyes wander to the left of the panel and you see a small grizzly bear wearing nothing but a blue bow tie. The small grizzly bear's face is frozen in shock, horrified by what the sickly grizzly bear is doing to the beehive. Between the two bears you see a pic-a-nic basket turned on its side, cash and pills spilling out onto a dirt trail. Your eyes follow the trail to the right side of the panel, past the unfolding insecticide, where you see a small trail sign that reads: Jellystone Park Refinery.

Yogi Bayer $15,000
Mixed media on panel, 48" x 48"   Sold

Small Bear: What are ya doing with that there flamethrower, Yogi? I don't think Mr. Ranger's gonna like that.

audience laughter

Big Bear: They started laughing at us, Boo-Boo.

Small Bear: Who started laughing at us, Yogi? I don't hear anything.

Big Bear: Hundreds of them, all at once. It must be all these here bees.

Small Bear: I don't think so, Yogi. These bees are just minding their own buzz-ness.

audience laughter

Big Bear: There it is again! Did you hear it, Boo-Boo! It was them ... the bees are laughing at us!

Small Bear: Noooo! Yogi, stop!!

Big Bear: I'm a-gonna kill all the bees in Jellystone and you can't stop me, Boo-Boo! Nobody can stop me ... because I'm smaaaarter than the av-er-age bay-er!

You see a portrait of two well-to-do men standing next each other, shoulder to shoulder. Their features are exaggerated, painted in a style normally reserved for boardwalk caricatures and political cartoons. On the left you see a grandfatherly man with little wire rim glasses, his hair sticking out at the side of his head as he flashes a fiendish smile. On the right you see another grandfatherly man, a small lock of hair sticks up, front and center, and he dons a subtle shit-eating grin full of unnaturally white teeth. Their eyes are alive and cunning. As you look at each of these sociopaths, you get the sense that they are looking back at you, one of them calculating the lowest price for which you will sell your soul, and the other considering the economies of scale related to the dismantling, reverse engineering, mass production and distribution of said soul.

Tweedle-C und Tweedle-D $2,500
Mixed media on panel, 24" x 24"

Ah, now in this tale we do evoke
The dev'lish deeds of the brothers Coke.
With wanton quest for wealth and power,
O'er the Earth they would hunt and scour,
High and low for a large deposit—
Oil and gas—to pilfer for profit.
Despite methods of modern technique,
Their tools did break and were prone to leak.
Gizmos and gadgets and big machines
Tainted the soil with tons of benzene.
Oh! Chemicals did spill, ooze and seep
Into the ground, going very deep!
In time, spoiled dirt and toxic water
Poisoned many a son and daughter,
Killing all the fauna and flora,
Opening that box of Pandora.
Much to our sadness and due chagrin,
These men ne'er accounted for their sin.
Coercion and political sway
Let these evil brothers have their way.
Why did these men run the Earth amuck?
'Cause rich psychopaths don't give a fuck.

You see an extravagant chamber fashioned from polished wood and marble. It's the type of room that could only be used for legislation, congressional inquisitions, partisan squabbles or other stately events of pomp and circumstance. The front of the chamber hosts a multi-leveled rostrum topped by a podium and, behind it, a large American flag draped vertically between two Roman fasces. You see that the chamber is occupied by a number of deranged elephants and donkeys that look like they got stuck in some stage of mutation during the process of anthropomorphism. The figures come in all shapes and sizes—fat and skinny, smooth and wrinkly, short and tall, male and female—each dressed in formalwear and standing among the horseshoe-shaped stalls of the illustrious hall. The semi-bestial-semi-human occupants have turned their backs on the flag as they look to the rear of the room, each of them poised and donning an artificial smile, as if a cameraman situated in an upper galley is taking a class photograph for some unholy yearbook.

The United Citizens of Dumbos and Benjamen $10,000
Mixed media on panel, 24" x 24" Sold

The lands of the Evil Empire were represented by groups of elders. Many of them were elected or appointed to their ranking by the people, while others were born into rulership, or seized authority by force. However the (il)legitimacy of their power came to be, these elders were entrusted with the duty to represent the people as a whole and to govern in the name of the greater good. Instead, throughout many lands, the elders were sullied by self-interest and corrupted by riches. Others were blinded by religion, or simply wanted to watch the world burn. At the inception of a land called The United States of America, the chosen assembly of elders was known as the Congress, and in later years they became known as the Parliament. They were the older cousins of The Pheds, but, with few exceptions, they were twice as dim and twice as corrupt. This chosen assembly turned its back on the majority of their constituents and discharged their duties in favor of one percent of the population. The assembly took counsel with certain sinister, non-human entities—Eenks and Ellellcies—conjured by The One Percent. These non-human creatures were formed from nothing and bound to no one. The people began to refer to the elected assembly, disparagingly, as The United Citizens—an epithet borrowed from a ruling by a fickle lawman, Sheriff Scotus, which allowed The One Percent to purchase the elders and to enact crooked legislation.

You see a kind-looking old man with white hair and horn-rimmed glasses sitting in a garden. A red conical hat sits on his head. His clothes are plain—a blue shirt draped above brown trousers. His smile is gentle and his spirit is calm. A stack of books rest beside him. The titles contain words like "power" and "class" and "occupy." Garden flowers bloom and tower above him.

Gnome Chomsk	$4,500
Mixed media on panel, 18" x 18"	Sold

You see a thin woman with blonde hair wearing a yellow Victorian dress. She's standing under the canopy of a jungle, her arms crossed in defiance. One hand clutches a notepad and a pencil. A camera is slung around her shoulder. Her eyes contain deep compassion and wisdom. In the background, the silhouette of a man, or a primate, swings from a vine in the jungle.

Jane the Good Porter	$4,500
Mixed media on panel, 18" x 18"	Sold

(Above) The People of the Sun will know of few heroes from our era. Among them, however, will be Gnome Chomsky, a celebrated intellectual and linguist who lived in the forests and the gardens. He rode on the back of a fox and could speak with all the woodland critters. He tried to warn his people of the signs and symptoms preceding The Great Collapse through his writings and lectures. But many mocked him and ignored his teachings.

(Below) Among the heroes will be a woman known as Jane the Good Porter, for she carried a noble and heavy burden. She lived in the jungle among the chimpanzees, studying their habits and social order. Her observations redefined what it meant to be human. She pleaded for the humane treatment of animals and the protection of nature. Sadly, the stewards of The Great Collapse did not heed her calls.

You see a llama with a fluffy coif
and a silly, peaceful grin on its face
sitting cross-legged in a wide chair.
The llama wears a pair of square
wire-rimmed eyeglasses. A robe
of golden yellow and dark red is
draped over his shoulder, much like
a toga. Embroidered on the robe is
the numeral XIV.

Dolly the Llama $4,500
Mixed media on panel, 18" x 18"   Sold

You see a Hispanic man with wise
eyes wearing a toga, standing on a
hill that overlooks a sprawling and
serene farmland. His head is donned
with a laurel wreath of grape leaves
and he holds a sign attached to a
wooden dowel. The sign has a black,
pixelated representation of an eagle
with the letters NFWA below it.

Caesar Chávez $4,500
Mixed media on panel, 18" x 18"   Sold

(Above) Another hero will be Dolly the Llama, a religious figure that travelled the world promoting values such as compassion, tolerance and self-discipline. He advocated for a philosophical and religious harmony among all people. Though his example was honorable, he could not convince enough of the Evil Empire to follow. And upon his passing, he was the last of his kind.

(Below) The People of the Sun will know of a great leader, a Caesar that was of the people and for the people. Caesar Chávez advocated for better working conditions for the farmworkers in the land of the Evil Empire, and he warned of the dangers of the use of pesticide products. He organized strikes and boycotts in order to capture the attention and sway the hearts of the people of the Evil Empire. And although he was able to effect positive change during his lifetime, the people did not continue to follow in his footsteps.

You see a white horse riding through an opening in the sky as if cast out of another dimension. On the horse is a horrible creature with the pus-white body of a maggot and the head of a man, save for the slime covered mandibles that protrude from its maw. Its disgusting body sits sidesaddle, and its several thoracic legs pull back furiously on the reins. The horse's eyes are wide and wild behind flared nostrils. You see snow white hair forming the cul-de-sac of classic male pattern baldness on the rider. It wears round eyeglasses and it smokes from a long black cigarette holder, a permanent sneer upon its face.

The Haalut Burton $7,500
Mixed media on panel, 20" x 20"   Sold

Book of Revulsion 6:1-2
[1] Now I saw the sky tear open and beyond the chasm I heard a monstrous voice, "Observe and testify as to what you see here."
[2] I looked. And lo, a white horse plunged through the rift. Sat upon it was The Haalut Burton, The Ravenous One; given to it were the tools greed and ingenuity, and it set out to conquer the Land.

You see a red horse tear through the sky as if banished from the place beyond. The rider is a silver plesiosaur and it wields an enormous medieval sword with one of its front flippers. The tip of the blade is engraved with a compass rose with a large N at the top so that the blade is perpetually pointed North, or up. Its long neck lunges forward as if charging into battle and its snarl exposes sharp curved teeth. The horse bears a full suit of protective barding, including a menacing chanfron. A fleet of armed drones flank the beast and its steed. Flying above it are jets with names that start with F and B, and silhouettes in the shapes of W and V. Tiny satellites twinkle in the sky.

Grummie, the Lockheed Monster $7,500
Mixed media on panel, 20" x 20"   Sold

Book of Revulsion 6:3-4
[3] From the celestial void I heard the voice, "Observe and testify." [4] I looked. And lo, a horse, fiery red, went out from the tear. Sat upon it was Grummie, the Lockheed Monster; given to it was an immense sword and all manner of airborne war machines and munitions, and it set out to profiteer and take peace from the Land.

You see a black horse ambling out of the split sky. You notice that the horse is malnourished. Its mane is dull and frizzy. Dried spittle lines its mouth. You can see the outline of its ribcage, and its kneecaps are wasted and bulbous, like those of an anorexic sorority girl. In the saddle sits a balding Black man in a black robe. He would appear distinguished if not for the sunken eyes, dry-cracked lips and sallow cheeks. Tucked into his waistband are a sickle and a set of shears. He grips a book bound with red leather close to his chest and in tiny gold print you see the inscription 35 U.S.C. 101.

The Man Santo $7,500
Mixed media on panel, 20" x 20"   Sold

Book of Revulsion 6:5-6
[5] From the rift I heard the voice, "Observe and testify." [6] I looked upon the torn sky. And lo, a black horse appeared. And sat upon it was The Man Santo; given to him were the tools of jurisprudence and chemistry, and he set out to blight the soil and rape the Land of harvest.

You see the pale horse. The sky-rider is dressed in a futuristic—or perhaps a very, very old—black military spacesuit, with matching gloves and cape. The rider has five heads aligned in a top row of two and a bottom row of three. You see the heads as follows: A man with a pallid goatee; he wears a white skimmer hat with a red and blue ribbon. A man with a wispy Fu Manchu; he wears a conical bamboo hat. A man with a pencil mustache; he wears a red beret. A man with a waxed handlebar mustache and chin puff; he wears a powdered wig. A man with a bushy beard; he wears an ushanka. The polycephalic rider holds the glow of a miniature mushroom cloud in the palm of its right hand.

Darth Lecter $7,500
Mixed media on panel, 20" x 20"   Sold

Book of Revulsion 6:7-8
[7] And then the voice from The Beyond raged, "Behold! Observe and testify!" [8] So I looked. And lo, an ashen horse emerged from the depths of Hades. Sat upon it was a beast with five heads, and it was called Darth Lecter; given to them was the power to spread economic conflict and sow indifference, and they set out to consume flesh and destroy nations.

You see the *chef d'oeuvre* of the exhibition—evident based on the sheer magnitude and epic detailed imagery of the painting. Inspired by Victor Vasnetov's famous apocalyptic work, the four equine and their riders traverse the sky under a blood red moon, escorted by the military drones and V- and W-shaped aircraft. The fiery glow of the skyline is beautiful, but the landscape is bleak. War machines are strewn about the lower landscape among the rusting rubble of a collapsed civilization. Twisted metal of crumbled buildings stretches upward. A mother pulls out her hair as she holds the corpse of a child. A man bites into the flesh of another. Dogs and cats feast on bodies littered in the streets. A river of blood weaves in and out of the scene. Tattered flags sit atop abandoned poles with nobody left to defend them. Futility sweeps through you. It was all so meaningful once, those flags—those symbols that united masses. Those banners that defined a way of life. Those bits of colored ribbon that inspired men and women to kill and to sacrifice.

The Four Horsemen of The Great Collapse	$25,000
Mixed media on panel, 36" x 60"	Sold

Book of Revulsion 6:9-10

[9] And I looked as power was given to the harbingers of The Great Collapse to spread conquest, war, famine and death throughout the Land. The riders turned brother against brother, and father against child. They commanded the beasts of the Land to turn against Man. The ground shook, waters turned and fields burned. [10] The sewers were lined with thousands of lonely suicides. Mothers clutched the lifeless bodies of children picked through the rubble. The voice revealed itself to me as The Black Emperor. I observed and I testify to you: These are truly the last days.

Tyler seethes and all at once his senses cease harmonious functioning. His ears fail to process the aggregate of white noise generated in the crowded room. Instead, they single out various sounds and conversations from around the gallery and rapidly tune between them as if scanning for active stations on AM radio. The track lights swirl above him and the horizon bobs and sways. He can't feel his legs and he wonders whether he's floating. His mouth goes dry and the smell of melting batteries curls his nose hair. His throat constricts as if with a slow twist of a tourniquet. The weight of the episode crushes down on him like being sucked into the deep down bottom of the ocean with no opportunity to acclimate. There's a high-pitched ringing in his head—the sound that pierces and rattles a soldier's skull after the detonation of a flashbang. The pressure inside him swells and just as he thinks he cannot withstand one more second, a chill rips through his spine and the sensory chaos terminates instantaneously.

Tyler looks to the entrance of the gallery just as Isaiah walks in.

Tyler is relieved to see Isaiah, but relief vanishes as soon as he recalls that Isaiah is to be blamed, at least partially, for his current lack of a cell phone. He marches toward Isaiah and launches into a reproving account of the event at Shawn's and Momma's house.

"Hey, your boy destroyed my pho—"

Isaiah cuts Tyler off by tossing him a new iPhone, still in the box.

"Here ya go. I heard about what happened and I knew you'd be pissed, so I took care of it. Just take it to the store tomorrow to activate it."

"Uh, thanks," Tyler says, stunned. He slips the box into his back pocket. Then, with skeptical inflection, "But how did you know?"

"Oh, uh … Shawn texted me," Isaiah says. "But enough about that, did they have anything interesting to report?"

"Yeah, they asked me to help them prepare tax filings next year."

"No, not about that," Isaiah says, his attention focused on the image on the front of the show card.

"Oh, right. They said the body traveled from beyond the dusk. What the fuck does that mean?"

Isaiah nods his head but doesn't respond to Tyler. He squints while reading the text on the reverse side of the show card.

"Hello? Izzy? What the fuck does that mean?"

"I can't tell you. You're just supposed to gather intel and report back to me, remember? What'd you tell them about the tax filings?"

Tyler shakes his head and says, "Nah, that's not for me anymore."

"Figured you'd say that." Isaiah finally looks up from the show card. "Did this motherfucker steal your idea?"

Tyler glowers.

"Yes. Yes, he did."

"Damn. It's not your week, is it?"

"No. No, it's not."

And just then, the motherfucker approaches the duo, having left behind his fawning groupies.

"Well, he doth appear. I'll let you two be. Ty, remember to activate the phone first thing in the morning. I'll be contacting you then. Okay?"

Tyler nods his head and Isaiah leaves to stroll through the gallery.

"Hey kid, I've been seeing your name in the news lately. How ya holding up?" Andrew asks, sounding genuinely concerned.

"I'm fine. And now I know why you've been so secretive about this series," Tyler says, sorely.

"What do you mean?"

The question agitates Tyler. "You know exactly what I mean! You stole the entire premise of this show from my piece book—"

"What? When did—"

"About a year ago," Tyler says, in an angry hush. "In fact, it was on the same day I told you about my graff name. Maybe that will jog your memory, motherfucker."

Like a father trying to soothe an upset child, Andrew says, "Calm down. Take a breath. Okay, I remember that day. Tyler, none of these paintings came from your sketchbook. They're all my own creations."

"Andrew, you stole the entire *premise*—the idea to illustrate satirical myths of the distant future—that was *my* idea. And now I can't do it without being called a copycat. That means all my planning and work this past year is garbage, you fucking thief."

"Look, I admit that I may have been inspired that day, but I didn't take a single illustration from you. Why would I dedicate the show to you if I thought I was stealing from you? That doesn't make sense."

"I don't know, and that doesn't matter. I have proof. All I have to do is bring in my book and the works-in-progress and show Lesley that I started planning a similar series quite a while ago."

"And what good would that do? Who do you think she'll side with? An established artist that brings notoriety to her gallery, not to mention money, or an up-and-coming nobody?"

The words sting Tyler and Andrew seems to regret having said them.

"Listen kid, I'm going to bring you up—in fact, who do you think convinced Lesley to show your unsold work upstairs tonight?"

Tyler doesn't respond. He just looks down, studying the cracks in the polished concrete.

"I can see you're upset, Ty. I'm truly sorry about that. If it helps, just think of this as the cost of doing business. The price of success. You're just paying your dues … like a protégé who ghostwrites for an MC."

"That's different and you know it. We never had an arrang—"

The quarreling pair are interrupted by a gregarious voice calling out from the balcony. "Ah, my loves! I'm coming down, you boys stay right there."

Lesley Devereaux descends the staircase in a blue and green sequin cocktease—er, cocktail—dress. Her silky gray hair is draped just below broad shoulders. She's taught and slender, and when she walks the whole of her body sways like a swan, or a salamander. Bare legs emerge from a short, serrated hemline and they shimmer as they stretch all the way down to a pair of Louboutin stilettos—she's the type of woman that wears designer heels for every occasion. And she has an eccentric, old money aura about her. It's as if the very atoms of her being operate with the presumption that their vessel will never know struggle. As if generations of privilege embedded in her bloodline have resulted in the encoding of a lavish DNA, which, bequeathed to her such as it is, compels her to exude an insouciant confidence. She speaks with an accent that's foreign to LA and native to nowhere in particular. It's not French or Greek or the Queen's English, but it has hints of each.

"Ah, my shining star and my rising star. Now, which one of you boys will be riding me home tonight?" she exclaims with a dotty giggle. "Oh dear, pardon me. I meant to say, 'driving me home tonight.' Do excuse me, this has been a spectacular opening and I've had quite a bit to drink."

She stands between them and takes them arm-in-arm. "So how about it—maybe both of you?"

Tyler glances at Andrew inquisitively, the prospect of a libertine tryst having caused him to momentarily forget their feud. But Andrew's face is unmoved and Tyler reverts to his previous indignant temperament.

"Don't look so serious, boys. This is a celebration … for you both! Tyler, my dear, have you been upstairs? Your work is almost sold out! Go and see for yourself."

"Thank you, Lesley, but I haven't quite finished relishing the brilliance of Andrew's pieces, yet."

Andrew glares at Tyler.

"Ah, yes, these paintings are magnificent, aren't they? Such an extraordinary thesis. Only one remains unsold—"

"Which was to be expected," Andrew interrupts, "nobody wants a portrait of them hanging on their wall … but I just couldn't resist."

Lesley and Tyler smirk in response to Andrew's comment, which diffuses the tension to some extent.

"Ah, there's Robert! Please excuse me gentlemen, but I must go speak with him." Lesley kisses Tyler and Andrew on the cheek. As she departs, she says, "Do be sure to go upstairs, Tyler. And we must chat about your next series very soon. I'll be in touch."

When Lesley reaches the other side of the gallery, Andrew turns to Tyler and says, "See. I told you things were going to happen for you. Just play it cool, kid. You'll be all good."

"Andrew, I don't have a 'next series' anymore. You fuckin' stole it."

"Look, this isn't the time or place to have this conversation. Come by my house Monday afternoon. We'll sort this all out, I promise."

Tyler shakes his head and looks away. "No. I don't think that's a good idea."

"Well, it's an open offer—think about it." As Andrew turns to head back to his retinue of flatterers, he pauses and says, "Tyler, do me a solid and stay away from Lesley … you know, romantically. Despite her earlier jest, we have a thing going on and I think I'm in lo—"

"You're in no position to ask for favors, Andrew," Tyler retorts.

"I mean it, Tyler. Remember, I know shit about you—shit you don't want to fall into the wrong hands … graff … Faye."

"Are you fucking threatening me?"

Andrew shrugs, and with the composure of a cleric, clasps his hands, bows, and backs away.

Betrayal by a mentor yields a confusing mix of emotions—not only dejection and anguish, but a strange feeling of guilt. Tyler stands in stunned silence, trying to make sense of it all. But his daze is interrupted by a soft slug on the shoulder.

"Where have you been all day?" Chloé demands. "I've been trying to get a hold of you. My car got repo'd and I needed your help. Why didn't you respond to my texts?" Chloé backs off upon noticing Tyler's disposition. "Geez, you look like shit. What happened?"

"Long story."

"So why didn't you respond to my texts?"

"I never received them. My phone got destroyed."

Chloé huffs, "Wow, you don't have to lie to me."

Tyler retrieves the iPhone box from his back pocket and flashes it in front of her. "See."

"Oh, well … then why do you look like shit? It's like you haven't slept in days."

"I don't want to talk about it. C'mon, let's beat the crowd and go to the bar."

"But I just got here. I want to walk around."

"Whatever," Tyler grumbles.

"Whatever," she quips.

Tyler positions himself in the front corner of the gallery, as far away from the purloined panels as possible. He leans against the wall with a foul look on his face.

Fucking thief. I trusted him. I shouldn't've told him. I shouldn't trust anyone.

Fucking thief.

I should expose him right now … cause a scene … spoil the night for him.

My work is ruined. I have no other ideas.

It's all my fault. I shouldn't've told him.

No … he's a fucking thief. Maybe all of his art is a sham. People need to know. Do it. Go to the balcony and shout it. Expose the fraud.

Tyler glances at the balcony and is startled by the sight of Faye leaning against the railing, peering down at him. They lock gazes and her eyes narrow. Her countenance begins to contort into that wild and unrecognizable physiognomy.

Oh, fuck this. I'm outta here.

Tyler exits the gallery.

12

Tyler sits on a stool in the far corner of Nowhere, stewing in grief and self-loathing as the tavern buzzes around him. The crowd steadily grows as the culturati make their way from the gallery to carry on the night in revelry, and a sensory chaos again descends upon Tyler.

A young man steps onto the open mic stage. He's wearing a denim jacket with little round buttons that contain various punk rock insignias pinned above the front pockets. He loosens the clutch in the middle of the mic stand and adjusts the height to his liking. He flicks the microphone on and tests it by tapping his finger against the mesh screen. A thud echoes through the PA speakers and he takes a deep breath. With a nasally pitch and in a purposefully slow tempo, he recites: The preacherman's got his sermon, he likes to watch you swallow / The bankerman's got his wealth, he likes to watch you wallow / The politician's got his platform, you'll hang from his gallows / Everyone's selling you somethin', it's best not to follow / Praise be unto Eleutherios, and blessed be Apollo.

Whistles.

"VoHé!"

"VoHé!" "VoHé!"

"VoHé!"

Chloé enters the bar. Tyler sees her gabbing and laughing with someone as the pair make their way through the crowded room. On closer inspection, he realizes that the someone is Faye. The room begins to swirl around him and he closes his eyes and rests his chin in one hand, his elbow propped up on the bar counter.

Two men take the stage together. The larger of the two men is wearing baggy jeans and a do-rag. The other is wearing khaki Dickies and he sports a shaved head and peach fuzz that might one day qualify as a mustache. The larger man takes the mic from the stand. With a swift and energetic rhythm, he spouts: Ay, yo. What to do 'bout the man with an evil plan put on this land to test us? / I wanna poke out his eyes with the fiery rod of great god Hephaestus / or condemn him to a slow death, feed him spoonfuls of Grade A asbestos / but do not let him walk free, do not let him think he bested us / hop him in a time machine, dial back the theme to wild west Texas / it was a simpler time, no formal law to mind, just local customs and general guidelines / drag him through the street, hang him high and dry, try him for his sins and various war crimes / but I do not have such a contraption to bend the bands of space to time elapse him / save that for the colorful books with rectangle bubble box quotes and captions.

The crowd claps and cheers and the man hands the mic to his compatriot, who launches into a rapid and vigorous flow: We are the denizens of dilapidated tenements / subsisting on minimums and government benefits / our jobs being taken by artificial intelligence / everyday is a struggle between progress and helplessness / as disparity augments with every passing election / the failure of politicians to petition the government / on behalf of the people instead of big businesses / assistance is rationed by motherfucking Republicans / fanning the flames of perpetual restlessness / it's time to rise and revolt and topple preeminence / allow me to reiterate if just for the emphasis / it's time to rise and revolt and topple His Eminence.

The rhymesayers take a bow and the crowd erupts into applause and spirited hollers—except for Tyler. Tyler looks like he's on the verge of death, slumped over the bar counter.

Jason sees that Tyler needs help and he tracks down Chloé.

"Hey, you need to get him out of here. Take him home," Jason pleads, half-yelling to be heard over the raucous crowd.

"What happened to him?"

"I have no idea. But I can't leave the bar. Please, just take him home and get him to bed."

"I … I can't. I don't have a car right now, and I don't think I can lug him on and off the train," Chloé says.

Jason tosses his keys to her. "Take mine. It's right outside. Leave the keys under the doormat. I'll pick it up later … and thank you."

"Thank you," she replies.

Chloé shuffles Tyler through the house to his bedroom. She turns his back to the bed and lets him drop down to the mattress. She exhales and stretches her back and shoulders before grabbing his ankles to pivot his legs onto the bed.

"You really did a number on yourself tonight," Chloé mutters as she pulls off Tyler's sneakers. She unbuckles Tyler's jeans and removes them with forceful tugs on each pant leg. "This is not what I signed up for." She pinches the top of each sock and peels them off his feet. "I can't go through this again." She stands over the bed and debates whether to stay the night. She lets out a deep sigh, undresses, turns off the bedroom light and slides into bed.

The events of the prior two days have taken their toll on Tyler. His mind slowly fades into much needed sleep. High amplitude theta waves drift through his brain ushering in the twilight of slumber. The physical vessel relaxes—muscles loosen, breathing slows—but the Self is still on guard. Like some sort of primordial sentinel, the Self surveys the chosen location to ensure that the vessel is free from danger during slumber. That is, danger of an external nature, for surely the threat of predators also lies within. At this stage, the Self can still sense a variation in temperature on the skin. It can still sense the fluctuation of light from behind closed eyelids. It can still distinguish between harmless sounds and those that warn of impending peril. The Self crouches and waits. And waits. And waits.

Reasonably satisfied with the environment of the chosen location, the Self retreats a little farther, tiptoeing backward in a final exercise of caution. Theta waves are interrupted by bursts of rhythmic waves known as sleep spindles and the Self abandons the sentry post completely. The Self turns around to find it's engulfed in the dense canopy of a foreign jungle, encircled by the irregular beating of tribal drums, as if proclaiming the commencement of some sacrificial ceremony. But despite the ominous beating, the rhythm begets tranquility in the vessel. The Self continues vigilantly through the sweltering jungle, brushing aside strange and colorful flora from its path. It braces as a guttural growl of an unknown beast cuts through the atmosphere from an indeterminable origin. The Self looks to its hand—or the equivalent thereof. A machete appears. It hacks through the vegetation with calm and determined swings of the blade. Body temperature decreases and heart rate declines in the vessel as the canopy opens up to the grey rippled sands of a dark desert dune. Delta waves like ocean eels emerge from the vegetation line and slither past the Self—were they following the entire time? Were they the source of the growl? The Self raises its knife-hand in defense. The machete is gone. The Self trudges across the murky grey ridges as hundreds of eels chaperone in winding and sliding locomotion. They drift. They glide. They swim until they reach the far edge of the desert plane. The Self peers down into an infinite abyss. The hundreds of eels gather and swirl in a fierce cyclone of sand and electricity. They transform into the likeness of a little girl with pigtails. She holds the Self's hand and smiles, revealing those jagged black teeth. In a soft, sinister voice she whispers "goodbye," then attempts to push the Self off the cliff and into the bottomless trench. But the Self resists and struggles to stay upon the grey embankment. The little girl and the Self tumble and roll along the sand as they argue and grapple.

Tyler thrashes in bed, his limbs flail and his torso tosses about. He erupts into somniloquy, screaming over and over, "I am SOBR! Not guilty! I am SOBR!"

Chloé stands horrified in the corner of the room watching the violent fit. Breath is all but robbed from her lungs and she whispers "sober" to herself. She dresses, gathers her few belongings and leaves the house in a hurry.

The girl overpowers the Self and she watches with that wicked smile as the Self fades into the black depths of the abyss.

Tyler's body comes to rest in a state of temporary paralysis and his eyes flutter behind closed eyelids.

The bedroom windows rattle as a ghetto-bird coos above the house in the night sky.

The Third Hymn.

The choir finishes the second hymn and the members again change formation on the stage. Tyler is slumped in his seat among the multitude, having surrendered to the grips of The Deep Within. Half of the choir begins the third hymn in melody and rhythm arcane. The other half joins in song solely during the holy refrain.

> We strain our voices
> making joyful noises to our god
> son of Semele, son of Thunderer
> wretched in the eyes of Hera, our god
> who is called Dionysus, our god
> who is called Bacchus,
> liberator from those who would snare us, and watcher
> of our city, Los Angeles.
> Our god! Bliss-giver, man-liberator!
> Our god! Ear-splitter, who hates the arrogance-filled!
> We rejoice at his feasts and
> in the delights of his wine.
> As he went under and returned,
> to save his mother,
> he sends us under to save us from ourselves.
> He bestows his gifts and we accept them
> in the madness of his dance—
> to speak with His Beloved beasts is a heavenly gift.
> Our god! Mind-freer, gift-giver!
> Our god! Leopard-rider, whose chariot is panther-pulled!
> Blessed are we who participate in the gods' initiations,
> Sanctified are we who partake in his mysteries.
> When the gods walk the Earth
> meddling in mortal affairs,
> he will become as a lion and deliver us—
> and we will follow him, to victory
> or to a righteous doom.
> Our god! Bull-horned and ivy-crowned!
> Our god! Freedom-bringer, who abhors the unjust-crowd!

13

Tyler wakes and feels the ache of having slept in a contorted position. One arm is almost completely numb from a lack of blood flow. He shifts under the covers and deploys the mobile arm in an exploratory search of the other half of the mattress. It returns having found no sign of life, not even the remnant of a balmy depression in the mattress landscape—Chloé's warmth and imprint long vanished in the night.

Feeling returns to Tyler's arm and he releases pent up energy in the form of a yawn that requires the extension and flexing of all limbs—the type of yawn that results not from exhaustion but from total rejuvenation. He rises and sets about his usual morning routine.

What happened last night?

I remember the exhibition ... Andrew, that motherfucker.

I remember going to the bar. The mic was on fire. I don't think I had anything to drink.

How'd I get home?

Chloé?

Yeah, Chloé was there ... and she was with ... Faye.

Oh, god.

Faye, what have you done?

Tyler fretfully searches for his almighty machine. He grabs his jeans and sees the bulky rectangular shape of product packaging in the back pocket. A deluge of recollection hits him all at once.

Momma. Shawn. Timberland boots. New phone. Isaiah's next assignments. New cell phone needs to be activated. What time is it? Fuck!

Tyler throws on some clothes and hops on his bike to race to his cellular carrier's nearest brick-and-mortar location.

Tyler types his name in a computer that organizes the customer service queue. He takes a seat on one of the hard plastic benches that, inexplicably, could only have been designed to promote discomfort and increase aggravation while waiting for assistance. Monitors hang from the ceiling, broadcasting a twenty-four-hour news channel, which is periodically interrupted by interstitials promoting the newest cellular products and services. Gadget prototypes are secured on tabletops that are strategically placed around the simple floor plan. The walls are festered— er, festooned—with plastic packaging containing plastic screen protectors and plastic cases and an assortment of other plastic accessories. Each dangling item is priced at an absurd mark-up. Fluorescent light blares down on frustrated customers and refracts off the variety of screens and packages. The glare is almost unbearable. Employees in blue shirts scamper around the store attending to customer demands and caprice. One customer is disputing a bill. Another is trying to return a useless accessory. And a prospective customer is talking through every conceivable configuration of service plans and discounts. Nobody in the store is happy. Everything is a sales pitch. Everything is plastic—especially the smiles of the employees.

Tyler turns his attention to the broadcast. Two stale white news anchors banter meaninglessly about current events, making sure to work in a certain political party's daily talking points.

AND NOW FOR A NEW DEVELOPMENT in a story out of Los Angeles regarding the search for a notorious graffiti vandal. Harold, you used to live there, I think you'll find this one particularly interesting. We go live now to Sandra Alvarez, reporting from affiliate KNBC-6. Sandra?

Oh, shit. The story is national now?

Fuckin' Sandra.

Thank you, Cheryl. This morning, police discovered the bodies of two male graffiti vandals along Interstate 10 near the eastbound onramp at Crenshaw Boulevard. Although the bodies were discovered in close proximity to each other, it's not clear whether the victims knew each other. What is clear is that a Loyalist faction calling themselves "HTK" or "Hail the King" has claimed responsibility for the killings. The group issued a statement on their ThraceBook page that says, and I quote, "We will kill all graffiti artists in LA until we are sure that SOBR is dead. If the police cannot find him, then we will." Magistrate Inquirer Isaiah Carver, who leads the LAPD's Graffiti Containment Unit, had this to say about the incidents (roll tape): "At this time, we do not believe either victim to be the infamous SOBR. And this incident will most certainly drive SOBR underground so that now we may

Huh, I wonder who they were.

Goddamn, this is serious.

never find him. Unfortunately, GCU resources will be drained from the investigation of the SOBR matter because we will now need to lend manpower to the investigation of these so-called HTK killings. I urge SOBR, and the person or persons responsible for the HTK killings, to turn themselves in." All of this, of course, is in response to what local authorities—

Ha, clever. Isaiah—always clever.

Nice touch.

What? No! No, no… go back!

Hi there! Have you seen the new Samsung Nebula 10? Check out the size of this screen! It's the BIGgest on the market! The video streaming is the SMOOTHest on the market. And the battery life? The LONGest on the market. Go ahead and try it out for yourself at one of our product tables. You'll be amazed, we guarantee it. Don't forget to ask a team member about our unlimited data packages and bundling options!

Ugh.

Big, smooth and long? Are they selling dildos here?

Oh, c'mon already!

—down crown on a billboard in South Central LA, a symbol that has been adopted by other graffiti vandals and Insurrectionist factions throughout the Southland and, now, throughout the Kingdom as well. Still no comment from The Office of the Crown on any of these events. Sandra Alvarez reporting for KNBC-6 in Los Angeles. Cheryl.

Saw that on the train. But it's spreading?

Harold. Back to you.

Thank you, Sandra. Cheryl, I don't know about you, but I find this SOBR character and other, you know, vandals that consider themselves to be *artists* like him— *Shut the fuck up, Harold.*

—or her—

—yeah, sure, or her ... to be absolutely detestable. And who's to say that these individuals who belong to HTK aren't simply patriots helping to clean up the *Patriots? Wow. Un-fucking-believable.* streets when the government fails to do so? And, uh, of course I mean the failure of *local* government.

I agree, Harold. I think—

Tyler's attention is diverted from the inane post-story prattle as his name is called over the in-store speaker system. Tyler approaches a girl standing behind the retail counter who is struggling to cheerfully wave her hand in the air.

"Hi, how can I help you today?" the girl says, with as much enthusiasm as a minimum wage worker in the customer service industry can muster. Her nametag declares "Junior Manager in Training" right below her name, which is Melissa or Valerie or something.

"Uh, hi." Tyler pauses, his mind preoccupied with the implications of Sandra's recent update. "Um, sorry ... my old phone broke, so I need to activate this one."

"Okay, no problem," she says, with artificial delight.

Tyler hands her the device and she asks for his account information. She initiates contact with the heavenly cellular network in a mystifying ritual of clicks and taps and swipes on the screen in front of her, a form of liturgy characteristic only of a high priestess—er, junior priestess (almost)—of the telecommunications industry. She maneuvers through the digital firmament in search of Tyler's god, but something goes wrong. The ritual was not right. She sighs and starts over.

Tyler raps his fingers nervously on the counter and peeks at the news broadcast out of the corner of his eye. The pallid pundits have moved on to an important story about a C-list celebrity's recent run-in with the law.

He looks back across the counter. Clearly something is still wrong.

"Shoot, I'm sorry. This computer, I swear," she says, as she feverously begins again.

Click. Tap. Swipe.

Tyler grows anxious and his fingers collide with the Formica countertop with increasing rapidity.

The girl pauses and glances up at Tyler, irritated by the finger-rapping. She squints and tilts her head. "Have you messed with your network settings?" she asks, accusingly.

Tyler shakes his head.

The clicks intensify.

"Are you sure? I'm not finding you in the system," she snaps.

The taps are voracious.

"Are you current on your payments?"

The swipes: ravenous.

"I think there's a hold on your account. I'm going to need to call my manager over for assistance."

"Listen, I really, really need to get—"

She cuts him off with the lift of a finger.

This is fire and brimstone from behind a Formica pulpit and Tyler is a sinner in the hands of an angry customer-service-junior-priestess-in-training. Tyler silently pleads and repents.

But at last! Mallory locates the cloud wherein Tyler's god resides and the clicks, taps and swipes temporarily subside.

"Never mind. Here we go," she says. "Let's see … It looks you're set up for automatic billing, so that's good. However, there's a replacement fee and a connection fee in the total amount of fifty-five dollars. Would you like to take care of that now?"

"Sure."

Tyler hands her a plastic card and she processes the atonement for the relocation of his personal deity's dwelling. She holds the new device in one hand and reads a series of numbers on the back panel. Then, in a final and roaring click/tap/swipe medley, she wrenches Tyler's deity from the heavens with the urgency of excommunication and implants it in the new machine. The deity inhabits the familiar abode and makes it almost exactly as it was before. And the hallowed service is concluded.

Selah.

"You're all set." She hands Tyler the newly consecrated device. "Just give it a few minutes to sync with the network and you'll receive any missed messages. Could I interest you in bundling with any other services today?"

"No. But, thank you."

"My pleasure. Have a wonderful day."

Tyler cannot leave the store quickly enough. As he exits, the pings of previously unread text messages ring out from the device.

Chloe
-Hey I need your help can you pick me up?
-Hello
-Ty, please respond. I need your help
-Ugh. Jerk

Sorry, Chloé. It wasn't my fault. I wish I could've been there for you.

Faye (redhead from bar)
You see Faye. She's naked and standing in front of a floor length mirror that leans against a bedroom wall. One hand holds the phone just above her naval, the other rests on her hip. Your eyes are drawn to her breasts, dotted by freckles and puffy coral nipples. Your eyes dart between

the colorful tattoos strewn about her body and then to the curly, orange landing strip that vanishes into a fleshy pink crevasse formed at the cross of her legs. The reverse image of her face stares right at you, her eyes having focused directly on the lens when the image was taken. Her lips are puckered and one eyebrow is raised slightly higher than the other.

-Want to play before the show?
-At least send me a pic of you. It's customary sexting courtesy to return the gesture, you know
-Wow, ignoring me? Asshole

Damn. No wonder she looked pissed last night.

+1 (305) 555-9387
-Hello Mr. Tyler K., I've seen your work and I'm very impressed.
I'd like to speak with you. Please call me at your earliest convenience. –Nick

Who the fuck are you and how did you get my number?

Chloe
-Ty, I'm sorry, but I can't do this anymore. I didn't know you had a drinking problem
-You were a mess last night when I took you home. Then you had a nightmare and you kept screaming that you were sober
-I went through this with a boyfriend a few years ago and I

just can't do it again
-I'm really really sorry. I hope
you find the help you need

Wait, what? I don't have a drinking problem. What's she talking ... oh, Chloé, you've got it all wrong. That's not what I was saying.

A lump forms in Tyler's throat. His chest swells and tightens. He immediately types a response.

-I don't have a drinking problem.
-You gotta believe me.
-That's not what I was saying

Tyler waits with bated breath, hoping that Chloé will quickly respond. Seconds feel like hours.

-I dunno, Ty. It was pretty clear
to me
-You have to believe me. I can
explain everything
-Let's meet up later

[...]

Chloé doesn't respond. Three dots appear on the screen in blinking in succession, and then they disappear—that infernal ellipsis that tells of a message commenced but never sent. Tyler waits and stares off in the distance.

Time stops at the sound of the next ping. But Tyler's hopefulness is dashed with the messages that follow.

Dizzy Izzy
-Morning sunshine. U need
to go meet Juan Guerrero at
Valenzuela Park on Arlington.
-Get there ASAP.
-He'll be at the picnic tables

-Ok but how will I know who
he is?

-He'll know who you are

                    -And why is that?

-Cuz ur gonna stand out

-lol

                    -Thx dick

-Aw don't worry. U'll be alright

-Just be respectful and only refer
to him as Mr. Guerrero

Tyler rides off to Valenzuela Park.

High up on a nearby tree, cicadas call out their shrill song—that droning buzz that tells of nearby courting, or looming danger.

Wait, no—that's just the crackling of high voltage electrical lines running across the sky.

The Fourth Hymn.

The third hymn comes to a close and the choir remains in position on the stage as one of the members steps forward from the back row. The member wields a large staff wrapped with ivy and topped with a pinecone—a thyrsus. He sways the thyrsus back and forth as indecipherable words of some unknown tongue emerge from behind his mask in deep, guttural harmonics—like a Mongolian throat singer performing at an intimate gathering inside a yurt. Tyler is in the grips of a trance, bobbing back and forth in the pew. A deluge of unsettling memories splashes into his mind. The voice of a little girl enters among them and although her words are within him, he is not consciously aware of them.

The man in black beckons
The man in black beckons
The man in black beckons
The man in black comes!
He sees you
He sees you
He sees you
And you see him!

Anxiety forms in the soup of Tyler's mind—the beginnings of a premonition of an impending doom. The sensation swirls around the confines of his skull and makes its way down his spine and slivers into his soul.

14

The metallic reverberation of trumpets and the faint squeals of children playing outside carry with the wind. And as Tyler nears the park, the sound of music being played at a celebration forms in the distance, instrument by instrument. Violins followed by an accordion. The rapid strumming of a *vihuela*. The plucking of a *guitarrón*. And eventually, rising far above the instruments, the melancholic cry of a tenor. The sounds twist and whirl together like ribbons around a maypole to form the rich and peppy texture of a traditional mariachi melody.

Tyler rounds a corner and the celebration comes into full view. Alarmed by the sheer number of people that have taken over the small neighborhood park, Tyler hops off his bike and walks with it at his side.

Barbeques and makeshift grills on small carts are scattered about the park. People cluster around each one and eat and drink while boisterously visiting with one another. Children run around a colorful jungle gym in a large sandbox in the middle of the plaza. The atmosphere is that of a massive *quinceañera*, but nobody is dressed up. The girls are not wearing fancy dresses and the men are not wearing suits. Only the band is in formal dress—outfitted in traditional *charro* attire.

As Tyler approaches the celebration, a number of male attendees stationed around the outskirts of the party make it clear, with intimidating stares, that Tyler is not welcome here—or if he is welcome, that he needs to watch himself. Tyler glances away and hangs his head, a signal that he's not looking for trouble, and he slowly walks on beside his bicycle.

How'm I gonna find Mr. Guerrero in this crowd? Or how will he find me before I'm chased outta here?

Tyler continues around the perimeter of the festivity. He spots a couple of picnic tables sitting in the shade of a large Magnolia tree at the far end of the park. The tables are separated from the rest of the party and appear to be occupied by a handful of stern looking men. And by the way the men congregate around the tables, lounging and watching over the celebration, it's clear that these are men who are in charge—men who are loved or feared by the rest of the partygoers.

Tyler sighs.

Here goes nothing.

Tyler makes his way to the tables. The group notices the approaching outsider and each of them dramatically shifts their posture. Spines straighten. Arms cross. Stances widen. If only human ears could noticeably stand alert—if only humans still had fur to bristle. Their conversations die and Tyler starts to sweat as he passes the point of no return—that certain distance after which turning away is no longer an option without first offering an explanation for his presence.

Please let one of you be Mr. Guerrero.

As Tyler closes in, he scans the group without looking directly at any of them. The first thing he notices is that they are not exclusively male. One woman is among them. Up close she has all the traits of a vibrantly beautiful Latina woman. From afar she was camouflaged among the men because she's dressed just like them—khaki slacks with a crisp crease, plaid Pendleton shirt, white Nike Cortez sneakers and a beanie. The second thing he notices is that—*Oh, shit*—the eldest man in the group is the *vato* from the train yesterday.

Tyler looks the *vato* in the eyes. The *vato* returns the stare and for a split-second his eyes open wide, exposing more white than he would have liked.

When Tyler is only a few steps from the table, the *vato* stands and strokes that thick salt-and-pepper mustache.

"You're Tyler?" the *vato* asks.

"Yes," Tyler replies. "And you're Mr. Guerrero?"

"Sí," he responds, letting the vowel trail out.

Tyler and Mr. Guerrero stand in silence for a few long seconds. The others, postured such as they are, wait with nervous anticipation for Mr. Guerrero to speak or to make some other move.

"Well, this is a twist of fate." Mr. Guerrero nods in contemplation. "Giros extraños."

Tyler doesn't speak. Nothing was asked of him and he recalls Isaiah's instruction—or was it a warning?—to be respectful.

"¿Está bien, jefe?"

Mr. Guerrero responds by lifting one hand and commanding, "Todo está bien. Leave us. Let us speak privately. Disfruta la fiesta. Todos ustedes."

The young men obediently turn and walk away from the picnic tables.

"Tu también."

"No, papá," says the woman.

Mr. Guerrero straightens his posture and cocks his head at the disobedience. Then he assents to the bold response with a slow downward nod. The same words from any of the other congregants would have come at great cost.

Mr. Guerrero resumes silent contemplation, as if mulling over some great paradox. Tyler and the young woman trade glances before Mr. Guerrero, having arrived at some conclusion, invites Tyler to sit at his table. Tyler flips the kickstand on his bike and the threesome sit down together.

"Magistrate Carver set up this meeting today, but there is no way he could have known about our interaction yesterday. Fate, indeed."

"Yes, quite a coincidence," Tyler adds.

"No, not a coincidence. Fate. Fate is the only word that can describe these circumstances. Let us speak of the events that occurred yesterday. Do you mind?"

"Um, okay."

"When you entered the train and you saw the marking of the crown on the door, something … exceptional … happened inside of you and travelled outside of you. Am I correct?"

"I suppose so," Tyler responds, reluctantly.

"No one on that train was paying attention, but I knew it the moment it happened. I saw it in your eyes. And I felt it, whatever it was, travel through me. In my life I have experienced this once before, many, many years ago. It came from a man that possessed much charisma. A man that inspired multitudes to follow him—for better or worse."

"¿Quien, papá?

Mr. Guerrero does not answer. He stares out for a thousand years—er, yards. Tyler and the young woman trade concerned glances once more.

"Look around you, Tyler," Mr. Guerrero continues. "Do you know why we gather here today?"

"A wedding … or a quinceañera, perhaps?"

The young woman looks amused. "Él no sabe," she says, under her breath, directed at her father.

"No," Mr. Guererro says. "But I'm glad you perceive this gathering as a celebration. That's the intended spirit. This is, however, less of a celebration and more of a farewell party. A farewell to a way of life. And for some of us, maybe even life itself."

Mr. Guerrero briefly pauses. "You don't know about the march?"

Tyler is slow to respond. "No, I don't think so."

Mr. Guerrero gives his daughter a side-glance of disbelief.

"Te lo dije," she responds.

Mr. Guerrero lets out a bitter huff and says, to Tyler, "You have the luxury of oblivion—you drink from the waters of Lethe."

Tyler draws a breath, the slightly exaggerated sort that often precedes a foolish or defensive retort. Mr. Guerrero silences him with the wave of a hand.

"Our people have been treated unfairly in this country for far too long—or a large segment of us have, that is—the segment that fills the gaps. The mechanics and the maids. The gardeners. The cooks. The busboys and the pickers. Life would not be easy for everyone else if not for us—if not for the laborers. Yet we struggle. We do not earn a living wage. Mothers and fathers work multiple jobs to survive. We cannot be there to raise our children. And our children go hungry or eat poorly. We are the recipients of police brutality and the targets of unfair laws. We are stereotyped in books and movies and television. When we are not being used as scapegoats by the politicians, we are pandered to and offered empty promises. I could go on and on. And it's only become worse since the *coup d'état*. We've had enough … I've had enough."

Tyler nods in a deferential manner.

"To put it frankly, black and—"

Ping.

"—brown are uniting. Tomorrow night our people march on the city to demand change. All are welcome—we hope our allies will join with us. Thousands—tens of thousands—will leave their homes on foot to march on downtown LA. We will sing and chant. We will—"

Ping.

Mr. Guerrero scowls in response to the disruptive sounds springing from Tyler's pocket.

"—beat on our drums and blow on our trumpets. It will be a peaceful event, although some will surely do their best to make it seem otherwise. Community leaders will interview with the media and state our demands. And all at once, the people will disband and return to their homes. We will protest in this manner for six nights.

"Of course, it's foolish to believe that there will be any immediate change. The point is simply that our people need to raise their voices, to let out their rage. Not everyone will agree with us. But differing opinions are just that—opinions. To live in a society is to live among innumerable opinions. But those who voice theirs loudly, and often, and in unison, will inevitably win. The act of protest and demonstration—and even riot and uprising—are necessary tools in the negotiation of the social contract. These six nights will mark the commencement of our renegotiation. And on the seventh night, if we have not been taken seriously, we will let out a mighty scream."

Tyler squints and cocks his head.

Mr. Guerrero smirks and says, "You don't need to understand. But know this … this march, it was planned to occur in the New Year, but we moved it up … in large part because of you. The public is captivated by your story and your symbol—your defiance. People are talking, the media is paying attention, and we think it's best for us to strike while the iron is hot."

A self-satisfied grin creeps onto Tyler's face. The young woman looks skeptical, or confused.

"This brings me back to fate, Tyler. We're going to carry banners with your symbol and your ... slogan. People will see that you helped to ignite this movement. You will be a hero to many, and a villain to others. You yourself will become a symbol—I've seen it happen before, and I think it's only fair for you to know before it occurs."

Flashes of a little girl with pigtails and jagged teeth cut into Tyler's mind like a strobe light. Tyler winces and faintly recoils with each flash. The girl laughs—a deep and sinister mocking. An air of dread flourishes on Tyler's face.

"Hey, are you okay? You look pale," the woman says.

"No. I don't want that—whatever that means," Tyler protests.

"By the looks of you, I wouldn't have chosen you," Mr. Guerrero offers. "But after observing what happened yesterday on the train, I think I see the wisdom in Fate's selection. There's nothing you can do about it now. It is set in motion."

"No, you can't—"

Mr. Guerrero turns to his daughter and says, "Hija, éste es SOBR."

The young woman releases the confusion from her face and smiles and says, "Ah, entiendo."

"No! Please don't tell anyone else," Tyler begs of the both of them. "Nobody else can know."

"It's too late, friend. This is Fate's plan."

"No, this is fucked up—"

Mr. Guerrero draws a breath and glowers at Tyler.

Tyler shifts his legs out from under the picnic table and stands up.

"—I don't want any part of this. Leave me out of it."

Mr. Guerrero sits steadfast, fingers interlaced and resting on the table—his face cold and resolved.

Sensing that any further plea will prove futile, Tyler turns around to walk away.

"What about Magistrate Carver's business?" Mr. Guerrero hollers.

Tyler pivots his head to listen.

"The victim was an ABC man."

"What the fuck does that mean?" Tyler asks, his tone thick with insolence.

"Just give Magistrate Carver the message."

Of course, more goddamn riddles.

Mr. Guerrero and his daughter watch Tyler return to his bike and ride away.

"¿Él se convertirá en el símbolo?"

"Al igual que el disparo que se oyó en todo el mundo."

After putting some distance between himself and the park, Tyler stops on the side of the road and checks the pings, hoping they came from Chloé.

> Lesley
> -Tyler I must see you this
> afternoon. Please come
> over at your earliest possible
> convenience.
> -3645 Lily Rd. in Baldwin Hills

Tyler rolls his eyes and slumps his shoulders.

A'ight. Let's get this over with.

The sun beats down on Los Angeles with relentless ferocity. Rays of light and heat infiltrate peculiar layers of climate in shimmering, hazy waves. On the horizon, the knoll that is the community of Baldwin Hills rises high into the sky, like a place that exists only in myth, or in the hallucinations of a desert wanderer—a Fata Morgana forever trailed by the crew of a condemned ship.

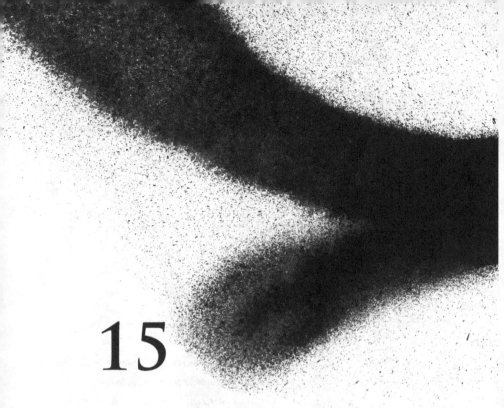

15

Situated on one of the winding streets in Baldwin Hills stands Lesley Devereaux's home—one of them, anyway. A temple of mid-century modern architecture and décor. Palatial by most urban standards.

The incline to the top of the hill is no friend to the casual cyclist. A serious cyclist, all clad in neon spandex, could stride to the top without breaking a sweat. But Tyler is no serious cyclist, and so he locks his bike to the perforated post of a street sign just off the dingy main drag of Rodeo Road—a street that's pronounced as it's written, without any pretentious accent—the way you might hear it in a pop-country song replete with bulls and blood, dust and mud, and the roar of a goddamn Sunday crowd.

Tyler embarks on the steep trek with Mr. Guerrero's words, and a distant memory, echoing in his skull.

We will beat on our drums and blow on our trumpets …

Beat on our drums and blow on our trumpets.

In a sea of drums and trumpets, you are a clashing cymbal. That's what Dehlia said all those years ago.

A clashing cymbal …

Or a clashing symbol?

Maybe that's what Dehlia meant. She was right about some of the things she saw. She was right about experiencing a loss ... my parents ... Katy ... I'll never love anyone like I loved her.

And she was right about having a gift ... it certainly bloomed ... or maybe I'm going crazy ... just hearing voices in my head. The march ... black and brown uniting ... is that what they've been talking about? Nah, this is all just a coincidence. Just a strange coincidence.

I'm losing it ... this is all so fucking crazy.

Shit ... Mr. Guerrero knows who I am. And now his daughter knows. It's not a secret anymore. And if more people find out, I'm gonna be in deep shit.

There's no controlling it now.

I gotta tell Chloé. She's the best thing to happen to me since Katy. I've been such a piece of shit lately ... but I can't let her go.

Fuck ... there's too much going on. I gotta stay focused ... gotta clear my name first.

Focus. Okay, what did Mr. Guererro say? The dead guy was an ABC man. What the fuck does that mean? Someone who works for the government? Like an alphabet man ... a G-man? Maybe he was FBI, or Office of the Crown?

Or maybe it's an acronym?

Always be closing ... maybe he was a realtor?

Tyler procures a list of ABC acronyms on his god machine. The search yields extensive results, a portion of which looks something like this:

Advanced Bionics Corporation
Agricultural Bank of China
Alcohol Beverage Control
Almond Board of California
American Bank of Commerce
American Blood Centers
American Ballet Company
American Beekeepers Collective
American Bird Conservancy
American Blimp Corporation
American Board of Criminology
American Bridge Company
American Botanical Council
American Bowling Congress

American Broadcasting Company
AmerisourceBergen Corp.
Anheuser-Busch Companies
Arab Banking Conglomerate
Archbishop of Canterbury
Associated Builders and Contractors
Association of Boxing Commission
Association of Bridal Consultants
Audit Bureau of California
Australian Broadcasting Corporation

Ugh, there's too many to try to make sense of it.

As Tyler rounds the corner of Lesley's street, he spies a purple BMW convertible at the end of the cul-de-sac.

The fuck is she doing here?

Tyler is seized by intrigue. He shoves his god machine in his pocket and scurries across Lesley's lawn. He brushes past white rose bushes, thick and overgrown, that guard the perimeter of the house like a curtain wall. He hunkers behind the bushes and scoots up to one of the small windows at the side of the house and peers into the living room.

There in the living room, Tyler sees Lesley seated on a sofa, gabbing away, but there's no sign of Faye. Lesley's gestures are large and animated and Tyler can almost hear her accent through the window pane. Faye finally walks into the room, her red hair pushed back behind one shoulder as she fiddles with the clasp of an earring. Lesley finishes with whatever point she's been making and Faye delivers a brief response, prompting Lesley to make a quick gesture with her hand in the shape of a gun while her lips form the unmistakable shapes necessary to proclaim "Bingo!" And suddenly everything becomes clear to Tyler. Seeing the two of them together in the house, going about their domestic routine, Tyler imagines Lesley's gray hair slowly filling with red from the roots to the tips.

Faye is Lesley's daughter!

And that's how Faye knew about the show!

Faye finishes clasping her earring and vigorously shakes her fingertips back and forth against her scalp to fluff her hair. She walks to Lesley, who is still seated at the couch and gabbing away.

Tyler ducks lower so that he can barely see into the room above the windowsill.

Lesley's lips stop moving and Faye's begin. Lesley bursts into that eccentric laugh that engages her entire body.

If only I could hear them. If only I knew what they were saying.

Lesley stands up to say goodbye to Faye and they hug as any mother and daughter would.

And then they kiss.

But it's not the kiss of a mother and a daughter at all, it's the kiss of lovers—carnal and intimate. Tyler's eyes go wide and white and he quickly squats down below the windowsill.

Who the fuck have I been fucking?

The front door opens and Faye skips down the brick pathway to her BMW and drives away. Tyler sits in the dirt, paralyzed by the implications of what he's just witnessed.

He sits and he ponders.

Not mother. Not daughter.

Girlfriends? Fuck buddies? Sure, Faye and I aren't exclusive, but Lesley … Lesley's with Andrew. Does he know about this?

Andrew. Fuck Andrew. I don't care if he knows. In fact, I hope he doesn't know. I hope this breaks his goddamn heart … and I hope I'm the one who tells him.

Ping.

> Lesley
> -Tyler dear, do let me know when
> you'll be here.

Alright, stay calm. What do I do? What the fuck do I do?

Tyler crouches like a sprinter at the starting blocks and peeks into the living room. No sign of Lesley. He scampers down the edge of the lawn back to the sidewalk and turns to head down the hill.

Ping.

> Lesley
> -I do hope you'll be coming
> soon. ;)

Tyler stops walking and looks up from the phone, considering for the briefest of moments the possibility of a hidden message in the text—the possible subtext. *A chance to get back at Andrew.* He about-faces and darts to Lesley's front door.

Standing on the brick patio under jasmine-covered eaves—perfectly trained and curiously in bloom—Tyler dusts himself off before chiming the doorbell. At the sound of the bell, a distorted human-like figure appears far beyond the rippled glass window in the door. The warped form slowly grows as it approaches. But for a moment, it stalls and changes shape—an amorphous blob behind the textured glass. Tyler knows it's just Lesley pausing to freshen up, or to slip on heels, or to put on lipstick before answering the door. But it all looks so hideous in his mind, like some amoeba feeding and copulating and dividing on a glass slide under the view of a microscope. Tyler looks away and all at once he regrets his decision to return to the house.

This was not a good idea.

I should go back.

Just walk away.

It's okay, she'll just think it was a solicitor that moved on to the next house. There's still t—

The door swings open.

"Tyler, dahling! I'm so glad you could make it. Come in! Come in!"

Lesley grabs both of Tyler's hands and brings him in for a kiss on each cheek. And she says, again, but with a sly chortle, "Please do come in."

He crosses the threshold and the door clasps shut behind him.

"Welcome to my home, dear. Please sit, make yourself comfortable," Lesley says, gesturing to the sofa in the living room.

Tyler sits down, intimidated by the impeccably decorated room. The bright white cushions on the teak sofa and armchairs. The shaggy white rug lying on perfectly stained maple hardwood floors. The white brick fireplace with a bouquet of peacock plumes in a clay vase on the mantel. And oh, the art! Picasso, Pollock and Lichtenstein on the wall. A metallic blue balloon dog by Jeff Koons on the coffee table. Brancusi's bird hiding in the corner of the room as if it's an afterthought. And is that a goddamn Matisse above the fireplace? The Dance?

I thought the only two of those were in New York and St. Petersburg. Must be a reproduction.

Lesley smirks in response to Tyler's puzzled face and says, "Yes, dahling, it's an original. The third in the series. The one nobody knows about. Henri painted it for me, pers"—she clears her throat and starts again—"It's *as if* Henri painted it for me, personally. Yes, I found it quite a while ago. Right place at the right time, I suppose. The owner didn't know what he had," she adds, in a bit of whisper, "And I had it authenticated under strict confidentiality.

"I don't tell many people about its authenticity, dahling. I hope you can appreciate that, and that you'll be discrete with this knowledge. And maybe one day you can tell me a secret about yourself, no?"

Tyler's eyes squinch ever so slightly in response to Lesley's last remark. He ignores the question, letting it remain rhetorical as was its likely design. He continues to look around the room with an air of bewilderment, taking in the wonderful treasures strewn about. But his delight in this moment is interrupted when one object in particular catches his eye. On the wall next to the front door, on a coat rack that may as well itself be a priceless work of art, Tyler spies a plain brown cloak hanging in definitive juxtaposition to a number of extravagant garments. Unmistakably, it's one of Andrew's cloaks dangling by the large hood.

The emotions from the exhibition last night rise to a boil within Tyler. Every fiber of his being rings with rage. He can hardly resist lashing out and telling Lesley about Andrew's theft. Andrew's breach of trust. Andrew's sham series.

But Tyler bottles it up inside. He strains his face so as not to show any emotion or any hint that he spotted the cloak. His eyes whip over to Lesley and he's sure she hasn't noticed anything. Her attention is unfocused—her gaze washes over the room as she admires her collection and savors the feeling, rare nowadays, of seeing it all through a visitor's eyes, so fresh and so new.

"Yes, I'm fortunate," she says to Tyler, or perhaps to herself. "I've acquired many remarkable works from my days in New York and Paris, and the wayward wonderings of my youth."

Lesley's eyes are honest and full of pining over days past. Friends, lovers and parties. Cigarettes and amphetamines. Poetry stained on paper in fresh ink from an Underwood typewriter. The Village. Montparnasse. Movements. Community—the type of which no longer exists in the era of Instagram and Tinder.

As her nostalgic gaze fades, she looks to Tyler and says, "But I'm, as they say, an LA woman now. This is my home. This is my fair city." She proffers some semblance of a smile.

Lesley sits down next to Tyler, her knees crossed and body angled toward him. She rests an elbow on top of the sofa and her fingers brush Tyler's shoulder. Then, as if that melancholic reflection had never occurred, her eccentric personality returns. "Anyhow, you're not here to live in the past with me, are you, sweet Tyler? No, you're here because we need to discuss your work. It's extraordinary and last night people took notice."

Tyler still has not said a word.

"Tyler, I want you to formally sign with me. An exclusive deal. For the next five years you paint for me, and me alone. You'll have unlimited resources and I will pay you handsomely. And if you keep your end of the bargain, you'll be rich and famous within two years—that I can promise. You and Andrew—they'll write about the two of you for generations to come."

Andrew.

Tyler cannot stay silent any longer. "Andrew stole my work," he says, coldly.

Lesley sighs. "Oh, Tyler. I was hoping you wouldn't see it that way."

Wouldn't see it that way? You ... knew?

Open the motherfucking floodgates.

Tyler jumps up off the couch and grills Lesley. "Are you saying you knew about it, and you didn't do anything? You went forward with the opening anyway? You allowed him to steal my work?"

"He told me the source of his inspiration some time ago, yes. You had an idea, but you weren't seriously pursuing it at the time and he was simply overcome with inspiration."

"He stole my idea!"

"Artists inspire other artists all the time. You, yourself, were inspired by Jheronimus, no? And anyway, one cannot steal ideas, dahling."

"That's bullshit and you know it."

"Do not tell me what I know, young Tyler," Lesley retorts. "I've been in this world much, much longer than you."

Lesley's tone is so comfortably lucid and callous that Tyler wonders whether her ordinarily aloof demeanor is merely affectation.

"All art is derivative. It's the amalgamation of every sensory perception in the artist's life," she says.

"I shared my vision with Andrew as a friend and a mentor. I trusted him."

"Yes, you chose to share a part of yourself. And by doing so, you inspired a passionate man. A man who could not sleep so long as the images were confined within him—images that you ignited, but images that you did not fuel. Did you expect him to torment himself forever by denying his need to express what's inside? The artist does not get to choose the source of the inspiration. You let something out and somebody else took it in. That's the way it goes."

"That's bullshit."

"Ah, yes. Again with the 'bullshit.' You're beginning to worry me, Tyler. Perhaps you do not have much creativity in you after all. Maybe I should reconsider my offer."

"Fuck your offer."

Lesley turns stone cold at the words.

"I will forgive those words only once. I acknowledge that you, too, are a passionate man, and that passion can blind reason and decorum."

Lesley rises from the sofa and stands face-to-face with Tyler. She's slightly taller than him in her high heels. She sighs gently and in a calm tone says, "I see that my point of view is not agreeable to you right now. I hope that that is only temporary, as I believe we have a wonderful future ahead of us. We will speak tomorrow when tempers have cooled. Until then, let me leave you with a single thought.

"Andrew is an established artist. He has given you much in the way of mentorship. It's why you had any work worthy of traditional exhibition in the first place, dahling. So, think of this situation as that of the ghostwriter and the famous author. You did the writing, but he put his name on the cover and thanked you in the Acknowledgements. It's the same with the rap music, is it not?

Maybe it isn't such a big deal after all."

The rap music.

Andrew fed her that line.

They've talked this through.

Lesley strokes a lock of hair poking out from under Tyler's hat.

"This is not how I was hoping our visit would go. Ah well, c'est la vie. I should ready myself for the day's affairs. Please feel free to take a moment to enjoy the work in this room. I trust you will show yourself out after an appropriate time. Goodbye for now, dahling. Be well. I'll be in touch tomorrow."

Ping.

Lesley exits the living room.

Tyler hastily glances from one priceless work of art to another, now unimpressed by it all. He walks to the front door and reaches for the handle. But before he opens the door, he again spies Andrew's cloak—it hangs there, right in front of him, mocking him.

Fuck Andrew.

Tyler takes off his hat and hangs it over the hood of Andrew's cloak.

Dwell on this, motherfucker.

Tyler leaves Lesley's house and descends the hill while responding to the recent text message.

Dizzy Izzy

-U need to go downtown and find
an unlicensed club. I don't have an
address but it's in the industrial area
and it will have a black gate with a
pink call box outside.

               -That will take forever.

-I'm sure you'll find it quickly. Don't
bike it, take the truck

-When you get inside, talk to Dale

           -And ask for what? Another
                 stupid riddle?

-Just do it

-And when you find the place, there's
a series of 3 passwords to get in

-Okay, what are they?

-Let's see…

-How can I explain it, I'll take ya
frame by frame it, to have y'all
jumping, shouting, saying it…

-What are the passwords?

-Izzy?

-Why did you send me Naughty
by Nature lyrics?

-Izzy?

Goddamnit, Isaiah.

Tyler reaches the base of Baldwin Hills and makes his way back to the street sign where he locked his bike.

"Fuck!"

His bike, of course, has been stolen.

Three. That's three this year.

Tyler calls upon his god machine to bid for a car. But as is often said, sometimes the gods work in mysterious ways. We knock, but they do not answer. We ask, but we do not receive. We seek, but we do not find. And thus, there are no cars available in Tyler's immediate area. Forsaken, Tyler is left to his own devices.

"Hey! Hey kid!"

Across the street, a boy in his early teens rides a beat-up fixed gear bicycle. Tyler catches his attention and runs over to him. A car swerves and honks as Tyler darts out in the middle of the street.

"Hey, how much for the bike?"

"What?"

"The bike … how much do you want for it?"

"I can't sell it. I need it for school."

"Just name your price, kid. You can buy a better one."

"I dunno, man."

"C'mon, please, I really need it."

"Three hundred dollars."

"Three hundred! For this?"

"You know what, forget it, get outta my w—"

"Okay, okay. You on Venmo?"

"Yeah. YungMerc07."

The god machines speak in ones and zeros and reckon the transaction. The kid walks away, a smile blazed across his face.

On his way home, Tyler passes a metal grocery cart overturned in a dirt planter in the sidewalk. The basket is brown with rust and brittle from decay as Mother Nature reclaims what is rightfully hers, leaving behind only the parts that have been stolen from her forever.

The Fourth Hymn (cont.)

The singer with the thyrsus begins to hop and shake and twitch, and the rest of the choir follows suit. They raise their hands in the air in the way that some Pentecostal Appalachian preacher might lift rattlesnakes in a misguided devotion—or a reckless dare—to his god.

16

Tyler weaves through the numbered streets of industrial downtown Los Angeles, in search of the black gate with a pink call box. The melody to "ABC" by The Jackson 5 is stuck in his head all the while.

Couldn't he just give me an address? I'm gonna waste all day looking for this fuckin' place.

The buildings in this area are all the same—giant blocks in various shades of dishwater gray. Each compound is surrounded by some form of wrought iron fence and barbed wire. Sheets of plywood hang behind broken windows. Designer brand names are stamped in tiny signs on the walls of some of the buildings, as if the signs themselves are embarrassed to be associated with such rudimentary architecture. Dirty cars fill the parking lots and line the streets—each appearing to be on its last legs. The owners of these dilapidated vehicles toil away inside the drab cubes. Some stitch and some sew. Some dispense and some receive. Few call and most row. All tire and all grieve.

Up ahead, Tyler sees a Pepto-pink call box fitted on a solid black gate. *Finally.* He pulls up to the box and presses the button.

"D.P. Manufacturing. Pick-up or delivery?"

Tyler stares at the call box, holding his breath as he takes a moment to think to himself. "Other," he says, laced with uncertainty.

The gate retracts and Tyler drives onto the compound. He pulls up to a podium with a sign that reads: Complimentary valet parking. Tips appreciated.

A little man in a white shirt and a red vest tears a ticket and slides one stub under the windshield wiper. He opens Tyler's door and hands him the corresponding stub.

Tyler steps out of the truck and the man says, "Whose country, my friend?"

The question catches Tyler off guard, but he knows the answer, lyrically and otherwise. After a quick beat, he says, "Peoples'."

"Sí señor," the man says, as he scoots into the truck and shuts the door. Tyler watches him drive off to god-knows-where.

This particular gray behemoth has one door at the center of the building and absolutely no windows. In front of the door, a red velvet rope droops between two gold stanchion posts, and a hefty bouncer in a black three-piece suit—half a size too small—stands next to it.

Tyler approaches the door and stands before the corpulent man.

The bouncer stares at Tyler.

Tyler stares back.

"What's your pleasure?"

Tyler smirks. "Pussy."

The bouncer makes a motion for Tyler to lift his arms. He runs his meaty hands across Tyler's arms to his collar, then down his ribs and around his waist, then down the outside of his pants and back up along the inseam, finding their way high up on Tyler's inner thighs. Satisfied, the bouncer unclasps the velvet rope and opens the door.

"Welcome."

"Thanks," Tyler says, in a borderline sour tone.

The bouncer's posture stiffens at the perceived disrespect and Tyler rushes through the door.

The door slams behind Tyler and he finds himself in a dark, narrow hallway. He makes his way down the corridor until he reaches a thick curtain. He shifts the curtain aside and is immediately assaulted by bright pink, blue and red lights.

Ah, it's THAT type of club.

Thin tubes of fluorescent light are arranged in geometrical shapes on the mirrored ceiling—assorted triangles, circles and waxing or waning moons. Posh bucket seats are set out around short cocktail tables. A fully stocked bar is positioned in the back of the room, and a semi-circular stage nuzzles up to one of the back corners—no seats around it, standing room only. The main attraction is a long, raised catwalk that splits the room in half, lined with multi-colored diodes like edge lights on a tarmac. Short stools flank the runway and three evenly spaced chrome poles emerge from the polished surface and disappear into the ceiling.

The vibe on this Sunday afternoon is rather low key, but it's evident that this den is accustomed to hosting a heavy volume of skin and dance enthusiasts.

The few patrons gather around the corner stage. The music is slow and moody. The lyrics are repetitive and unintelligible, as if the words themselves are drowning in a cup of codeine. A bikini-clad woman on the stage sways to the narcotic groove, her back pressed against a shiny pole.

Tyler makes his way over to the stage and a young man approaches him.

"Can I get you a drink, sir?"

Tyler shakes his head and offers his thanks.

"Perhaps something more intimate then?"

Again, Tyler shakes his head and offers his thanks. The young man walks away disappointed.

"Hey, I'm looking for Dale," Tyler calls out.

"Keep looking," the young man quips.

Tyler turns his attention back to the stage. The dancer is hanging upside down with the pole gripped tightly between her powerful thighs. She pulls the string of her bikini top and lets it fall to the ground. Patrons toss small denomination bills on the stage floor.

The dancer grips the pole with two hands and hoists herself all the way to the ceiling. At the top of the pole, she again flips herself upside down. She grabs the pole beneath her and spreads her legs wide, then slowly spins down, like a helicopter shot out of the sky. A patron throws a band of dollar bills into the air and they rain down upon her like New Year's Eve confetti, or napalm.

The routine is over. The dancer collects her gains and disappears behind the stage.

Tyler looks around the room and can't seem to identify anyone who actually works there. Nobody is behind the bar. Nobody is wearing a uniform. Nobody is working the floor. And he's not quite sure if that young man was an employee or a guest—perhaps a freelancer, of sorts.

Tyler sits and waits. He's here to see Dale because Isaiah instructed him to do so—certainly Dale must be expecting him.

Another song. Another dancer. Another routine.

Tyler begins to zone out while letting his mind wander, when suddenly there's as tap on his shoulder. Tyler turns and immediately recognizes the woman as the first dancer, even though she's now right-side up.

"I'm Dale," the dancer says.

Tyler fumbles with his words before finally saying, "Hi, I'm Tyler."

Dale smirks. "Come with me."

Dale leads Tyler across the room, the tail of her silk robe flowing behind her. They pass through a velvet curtain and enter a hallway that splits into several stalls, each of which is shielded from the corridor by a screen of beads.

The beads chime like a New Age instrument as they enter the stall farthest down the hallway. The space is awash with red light and a chaise lounge sits in the center of the room.

"Have a seat," she says.

Tyler obeys.

"Izzy tells me you're a believer. That you practice the old ways."

Izzy? She knows him well enough to call him Izzy?

"Uh, yeah, I try to … when I can."

Dale is a little disappointed with the answer.

"He tells me you're special."

"That's nice of him."

"I think he's probably right. I could feel your energy when you walked in. That must mean you've known my kind."

"Your kind? And what would that be?"

"I've got old blood in me—the kind that sees," Dale says. "Let's see what it tells me about you."

Tyler starts to stand and says, "You mean you want to read me …
no, I've done that before. I don't think it's such a good ide—"

Dale pushes him back against the chair. "Relax," she whispers.
She turns to a small panel on the wall. Click, tap, swipe and suddenly
there's a buzzing that comes from the ceiling. The buzzing swells
and sounds like it's moving around in a circular motion above them.
A drumbeat kicks in and The Weeknd's sultry tenor floats down to
Tyler and Dale, like a tired balloon at the end of a long party.

Dale faces Tyler and begins to move rhythmically. Wide hips
swaying slowly from one side to the other, like a galleon rolling in
the calm of an open sea.

Tyler is mesmerized as his eyes follow the flow of her body.

She puts her hands on the nape of her neck and with the very
tips of her fingers she brushes the robe from her shoulders and
twirls away from Tyler.

Her knees bend. Her hips dip and sway and tell no lies. Her
backside moves in sweeping ellipses as if orbiting some unseen astral
body. Each motion is purposeful. Methodical. Designed to enchant
the onlooker. For in these secluded backrooms, it's the serpents that
hypnotize the handlers.

Her arms stretch above her head, olive skin gleaming in the red
light. Ellipses. Perhaps she's enacting the solution to some furtive
mathematical formula, the kind the ancients discovered eons ago
when they stared at the heavens—long since forgotten. Ellipses. The
kind of formula if deciphered, and if mapped and modeled by some
stellar cartographer, might just reveal the true face of our creator.
Ellipses.

She backs into Tyler, spreading his knees and nuzzling into his
v-shaped legs. Ellipses. She places his hands on her thighs. Ellipses.
She arches her back and presses her cheek against his. She takes his
hand and offers him the tie to her bikini top. Ellipses. He tugs on the
string and the bow unravels. The cloth slides down her stomach and
falls to the floor. Tyler stares down the hollow formed by the divide
of her breasts—a locket looped around a gold chain rests between
them. Ellipses.

Dale snaps open the locket. Her finger dips in a waxy substance
and she sticks it in Tyler's mouth, rubbing the wax along his gums

and down his tongue. Then she does the same to herself. Ellipses.

Dale throws herself forward so that her head is between her knees—and his. The move surprises Tyler and he grips her waist to prevent her from falling. She places her hands on the floor and brings each knee onto the lounge chair, her ankles secured around Tyler's waist. Ellipses.

She maneuvers back to the cheek-to-cheek position, still sitting in Tyler's lap. Ellipses. She twists her body and lifts one leg high in the air and spins around so that they're face-to-face.

Tyler relaxes, loosens up. He slides his hands up and down her back. Ellipses. He begins to move in rhythm with her—now he's getting it.

The electricity between them intensifies. She pulls off Tyler's shirt. They flow together as one. Rhythmic moving becomes ecstatic dancing. Tyler retreats into himself. They lose consciousness. Ecstatic dancing becomes uncontrollable gyrating. Their eyes become an opaque glaze. Uncontrollable gyrating becomes possessed writhing. They lose themselves in divinity, in the purity of vacant consciousness.

... ...
... ...
... ... *tell the world* ... *tell Chloé*
... *I'm innocent* ... *declare it* ... I
am SOBR ... *strike back* ... A sudden flicker
of a little girl in pigtails ... *the man in black* ... *strike the*
only way I know how ... *get up and stay up* ...
... ... *long live SOBR* ... ... *tonight*
...the little girl smiles ... *the man in back beckons* ...
the overpass ... ... *he sees me* ... *bomb the*
overpass ... **Ping** ... sharp, black teeth in the
mouth of the child ... *the man in black awaits* ... ...
...*and I see him* ... **Ping** ... ...
... ...

Tyler rests on the floor against the lounge chair. Dale lies against Tyler. And the high of the trance gradually dispels as The Weeknd's final, repetitive lyrics drone to a close.

"Izzy was right. You have an odd energy in you," Dale says. "It's powerful and it's brimming ... like you're about to pop. I haven't felt anything like it before."

"That was amazing," Tyler says, dumbstruck. "What's in the locket?"

"Just an old liniment. Let's call it an old family recipe. But listen, my blood tells me you have a gift. It's speech of some kind. Your words, or your ears … you … you give a voice to the voiceless … to…"—Dale looks confused, then adds with an air of surprise—"to His Beloved."

Tyler winces at her words—at the accuracy of her intuition.

"I have to go," Tyler says, abruptly. He stands, throws on his clothes. "But I'll come back."

"I know," she says, somberly. Tyler wonders which of his statements elicited such a response.

"Before I leave, do you have information for Isaiah?"

"Yes—the victim was an enemy of our revelry."

Right. More goddamn riddles.

"It was good to know you, Tyler."

Tyler half-smiles at the ominous compliment. He takes a last look at Dale, lying nude on the lounge chair, then disappears behind the beaded screen.

Outside the pleasure house, Tyler stands next to the giant bouncer while he waits for his truck to be driven back from god-knows-where. No small talk is welcome—that's clear from the bouncer's mad-dog stare.

Tyler consults his deity.

> Dizzy Izzy
> -When you're done at Dale's, go
> straight home and stay there
> -Seriously, don't go anywhere.
> The diesels are out. A lot of
> them

The valet arrives and keeps the engine running while he scoots out of the car. Tyler pockets the god machine and hands the valet a few dollars.

He drives home—focused, confident, one goal in mind.

And the goddess Nyx emerges from her cave at the far edge of the ocean to dance with her daughter for a few magical moments before they bid each other farewell.

Day turns night. Day turns night. Day turns night.

Tyler parks his truck curbside. He enters the house and quickly makes his way to his room, avoiding the living room where a congress of his housemates and their friends, and friends of their friends, convene as the stern one leads a lecture.

"Americans have been sold a great lie—that their way of life is the essence of freedom. That their systems are the best in the world. That they are Number One. And so the people desperately cling to their systems and espouse their superiority with an ignorant fervor, like that of a child raised in a doomsday cult.

"But the reality is that no economic or governing system is so perfect that it is meant to withstand the test of time. To think so is to believe in absolute constancy—that there are no fluctuating variables on Earth that may interfere with the healthy operation or the good intentions of such systems. Nothing could be farther from the truth—existence is a sequence of ever-changing variables. And so an economic or a governing system that was suitable for a certain period of time may not be appropriate for another period. Thus, the task becomes anticipating the need to change the systems, identifying the form of change, and effectuating it.

"I will suggest that if Americans—ahem, if humankind—should voluntarily adopt a selfless way of life and embrace a system of democratic socialism that includes robust environmental regulations and family planning principles, perhaps this world could yet be saved. But I fear that by the time humankind comes to this realization, it will be too late. Socialism joined with a strong defense of nature and responsible procreation is a wonderful notion only if it is not the product of necessity. Once it becomes essential to survival, it is something else entirely—vulnerably close to authoritarianism. And in any event, as previously surmised, if someone was to call for this change, I doubt anyone would sincerely listen."

The crowd murmurs in agreement.

Tyler grabs a couple of cans of spray paint and heads out the back door. He paces down the driveway, retrieves the recently acquired bicycle and unlatches the gate. He rides out onto the street and into the urban nocturne.

Elsewhere in the city, an obsolete pay phone, all scratched and stickered, leans against a grimy brick building. The receiver dangling and swaying in the breeze.

The Fourth Hymn (cont.)

The guttural chanting intensifies. The chorus gyrates and wails.

17

The marine layer lingering over the Pacific Ocean strides toward the shore. It halts at the coastline as if hesitating to tread over dry land. With each indecisive second, a dense billow grows, forming a misty wall that towers over the Los Angeles basin. The foggy mass prods and pokes at the mainland with little vaporous tendrils, working up the courage to leave the sea. The towering fog finally reaches critical mass and all at once the great billow spills onto the land.

Tyler can barely see ten feet in front of him as he pedals through this cloudy mix of mist and pollutants. Cars emerge from the fog without warning and glide by like alien vessels on a desolate interstellar highway. Streetlights appear as UFOs hovering somewhere above him. The eerie scene goes virtually unnoticed by Tyler as he's single-mindedly focused on the task at hand—executing a daring declaration of innocence.

Tyler brakes and dismounts on a street that passes over the 101 Freeway. He lets the bike fall against the tall curb and he walks to the railing. He grips the thick guard rail, displacing beads of dew that had convened on a film of dark, oily grime. He leans over the side of the bridge directly above the center median, searching for the giant green traffic sign connected somewhere below the railing. On the highway below him to his right, red orbs in sets of two zoom away from the bridge. To his left, pairs of white orbs form in the distance and race furiously toward him.

Tyler centers himself at the sign located above the oncoming traffic. He throws a leg over the railing and straddles it like gymnast on a pommel horse. He pulls his other leg over and carefully lowers himself down into the jungle gym of bolts and bars and brackets that harness the sign to the steel and concrete bridge. His left foot slips as it searches for a firm hold and every muscle in his body seems to flex all at once to steady his balance.

Fuck.

Sweat drips down the baluster. Adrenal medulla dry heaves.

Tyler reaches the bottom of the traffic sign. There's not another foothold between him and the highway. *Now or never.* He steps out from behind the sign and onto the flange of a steel girder that runs along the bottom of the bridge. His fingers cling to a lip in the concrete at his eye line. He methodically slides along the girder toward the center of the bridge, inches at a time—left foot, left hand, right foot, right hand, left foot, left hand, right foot, right hand.

He makes his way just past the center of the bridge and retrieves a lone can of white spray paint from his back pocket. He holds the can in his right hand and gives it two firm shakes. He bends his knees and dips down to start writing in bottom-to-top fashion. Ah, that cathartic hiss of the spray can. The knuckles on his left hand go white as he holds on to the concrete lip for dear life. The first Tyler-sized bubble letter is written on the side of the overpass and he scoots an inch toward the traffic sign—right foot, left hand, left foot. He throws up another bubble letter and repeats the process with the diligent patience of a surgeon suturing a gaping wound. Another letter. Scoot. Then another letter. Scoot.

Tyler's progress is momentarily interrupted when a sudden shiver rips down his spine. He pauses to reflect on the curious sensation, but it quickly fades.

A'ight, time to wrap this up.

Tyler resumes writing the last bubble letter then tags his

pseudonym at the top corner. He pockets the spray can and makes his way toward the traffic sign.

Pop!

But before reaching the traffic sign, that all-too-common sound of a gunshot rings out, followed immediately by the matted sound of a ricochet off concrete. Tyler double-times it along the girder—right, right, left, left, right, right, left, left—and just as he reaches out to grab hold of one of the bars behind the sign—

Pop!

—another gunshot. This time the bullet hits the traffic sign with a metallic thud, and Tyler catches a glimpse of a muzzle flash in the fog to his right, somewhere in the foliage on the sloped embankment next to the freeway. He maneuvers behind the safety of the sign and crouches down as far as he can. He looks up and notices a faint beam of light passing through a small round hole in the sign—the sheet metal having curled away from the hole as the result of a violent puncture.

Fuck!

The backside of the traffic sign offers no refuge. Adrenal medulla hurls and surrenders to the clutches of shell shock. Good night, sweet prince.

Pop! Pop!

Tyler flinches with each clack and waits for the bullets to strike the sign. But the metallic thuds never come, and it occurs to him that this rapid fire didn't sound quite the same as the previous gunshots, and perhaps they came from a different direction—above him?

Okay, maybe the shots are not meant for me … maybe I'm just caught in the middle of some sort of turf war.

Tyler hunkers down and a few seconds of silence go by.

Reflexes … gotta make a move!

He stretches an arm above his head to start to climb up—

Pop!

—but a bullet pierces the sign and his arm instinctively recoils.

Oh fuck oh fuck oh fuck! Bacchus! Help me!

Panic sets in. Tyler looks from side to side, but there's nowhere to go without exposing himself to the shooter—or multiple shooters. He looks down and considers the drop, but he's deterred by that nexus where white orbs turn red. *No, not this time. Not here.* He looks up. It's his only option and he's got to be quick about it.

As he climbs without incident, his eyes focused on the railing above, he begins to hope. *I got this. Almost there. Almost there.* But just as he's about to emerge from the top of the traffic sign, a silhouette appears at the railing. Defeat washes over him. He stops climbing. His body sulks and he closes his eyes.

Pop!

Another metallic thud rings out beside him, and the silhouetted figure above him yells, "Tyler! What the fuck are you doing? Keep climbing!"

Tyler's eyelids burst open—*Isaiah?*—and he watches as the figure above him returns fire toward the freeway embankment.

Pop! Pop!

"C'mon, we gotta go!" Isaiah shouts.

Tyler reaches the bottom of the baluster and hoists himself to the top of the guard rail. Isaiah pulls at the collar of Tyler's hoodie, his left hand still pointing the gun in the direction of the embankment. Tyler rolls over the railing and falls to the sidewalk.

Isaiah paces backward and barks, "Get up and run, fool!"

Tyler jumps up and hops on his bicycle. Isaiah takes a few more backward steps then lowers his gun and dashes behind Tyler.

Tyler reaches Isaiah's Chevy El Camino and he carelessly tosses the bike in the pickup bed. Isaiah winces at the sound of the crash.

Tyler whips open the passenger door and slides into the car. Isaiah is quick to the driver's seat and he glowers at Tyler as the engine roars alive.

Tyler shrugs his shoulders as if to say, "what gives?"

"Inconsiderate fuck."

"Dude, we're running from gunfire!"

Tires screech as Isaiah skids into a U-turn in the middle of the street and speeds away, a swirl of smoggy mist left dancing in their wake.

Isaiah monitors Tyler out of the corner of his eye as he drives with one hand at the top of the wheel.

Tyler is lost in thought. The dots are exposed and he's slowly connecting them.

"How the fuck did you know where I was?"

Isaiah flashes a grin. "Think about it."

Tyler shakes his head in disbelief and says, "My fucking cell phone."

Isaiah simply nods.

For where your cell phone is, there you will be also.

"So you've been illegally tapping my phone," Tyler says, with disdain.

"Illegally?" Isaiah scoffs. "Don't be stupid, Ty. You know the rules have changed. The people don't have rights anymore—just the illusion of rights. If I wanted to know where you were at, I wouldn't need to *tap* anything, I could just buy the information … kindly made available for sale by any number of apps on your phone. And anyway, I saved your sorry ass, so you should thank me for *tapping* your phone. Ah, but hold up, it's not exactly *your* phone, is it?"

Tyler's face creases with displeased realization.

"That's right, motherfucker. I gave you that phone. I didn't need to go through any official process or use any official resources or buy any information to keep an eye on you.

"You were supposed to go home and sit tight after seeing Dale. Those were my instructions. But on *my* phone, I watched a little blue dot that represents little, disobedient Tyler—I watched it go home and then immediately go out again, which I knew could only mean trouble. So I set out to find you. I was just gonna scare you—teach you a lesson. But look what I happened upon—good thing I was watching your punk-ass."

"You betrayed my privacy."

"You're unbelievable. I may have betrayed your privacy, but I was faithful to *you*. Every beat cop in LA is looking for you tonight. Diesels are roaming the streets. Loyalists have sworn to hunt you down—some of those lunatics are killing graff writers indiscriminately. The media is digging for information on SOBR— and they *will* find something, eventually. There's a goddamn price on your head, and who knows who else you've pissed off.

"Yet you insist on runnin' around trying to solve your own case and I'm helping you like a damn fool. And you've been irresponsible for quite a while now—way before this whole thing started. You act is if you don't care whether you live or die. But I do care, Tyler. So if I decide that it's in your best interest to monitor your phone for your safety, as your best friend, that's what I'm gonna do."

"For my safety?" Tyler huffs. "Man, you sound like *them.*"

The comment stings Isaiah. Isaiah knows that Tyler's not wrong, but he's not exactly right, either.

"Whatever, man. What'd ya write out there, anyway?"

"Nothin'."

"Guess I'll have to wait to see it on the news tomorrow."

"Guess so."

Isaiah lets out a sarcastic snort in protest of Tyler's pettiness. "I hope it wasn't something obvious, like 'not guilty' or some shit."

Tyler sneers and turns away, staring off into whatever lies beyond the passenger side window.

And just then, they hear the knocking—that rumbling combustion of ignited diesel. They both go stiff, even Isaiah. Even Isaiah who, despite being police, knows his position as Magistrate Inquirer would get him only so far in any sort of confrontation with those who patrol in a Humvee. They hold their collective breath as the armored cabin-on-wheels appears ahead of them and rambles by. Breath remains walled up in the cask of their lungs until red taillights disappear from the El Camino's rearview mirror.

They each let out an easy sigh and a moment of silence drifts by.

"You can keep the phone, by the way. I can track it, but otherwise it's clean. I had our tech guy scrub it on the sly. But you really shouldn't carry these things with you anymore when you go bombing … only a matter of time before they catch you that way." A cynical tsk limps out from behind Isaiah's lips. "When Orwell and the old futurists warned us of technology that would be used to surveil us, I don't think they could've ever imagined how willingly we would invite it into our daily lives. We greeted the screens and the cameras and the microphones with open arms and invited them into our homes as houseguests whose welcome could never be outstayed."

Tyler's mind having wandered elsewhere, he suddenly barks, "Who was shooting at me then?" A follow-up question in a conversation that Isaiah was not, as of yet, privy to.

"How the fuck am I supposed to know? Probably some crazy-ass Loyalist, or some bum in need of an extra fifty g's."

"Fifty!"

"Uh, yeah, they raised reward this afternoon. You didn't hear?"

Tyler shakes his head in disbelief. He begins to offer another theory, "Or it was— "

"No, not the same people who framed you. For the last time. That. Didn't. Happen."

Tyler rolls his eyes up and the passenger-side window down. He dangles his hand in the breeze and stares at the shifting cityscape as they cruise into his neighborhood.

Somewhere nearby, tucked away under the cover of fog, a house party is underway. And the chorus of that most exalted modern dithyramb can be heard.

Over the centuries, as cultures collided and customs diluted, the dithyramb evolved and assumed the musical styles of the times. In this time and place, the ancient sound of the *aulos* has been replaced with the sound of a synthesizer producing that high-pitched G-funk lead. The song of the choir has been replaced with flow of the MC. And the dance of the sikinnis and the antistrophe have been replaced with the likes of breakdancing and C-Walking. But the funky rhythms, the enriched wordplay and the narrative storytelling still remain.

The chorus travels defiantly through the night sky, cutting through fog, competing with the rumble of the Chevy's engine, arriving at Tyler's ear as hardly a whisper, but powerful enough to compel a physical response—a testament to the enduring nature and influence of the song. Tyler bobs his head as the lyrics tell the story of a man strolling down the street, indulging in indo, and enjoying a cocktail: gin mixed with juice.

Isaiah stops the car in front of Tyler's house.

"This is almost over, Ty. You need to chill out and stay home. Tomorrow's a big day for us. I'll be in touch."

"Whatever you say, big brother." Tyler slams the door.

Isaiah scowls. Tires screech.

Tyler calls out, "Hey! Wait! My bike!"

But his voice is drowned out by the sound of the howling engine.

Ah, fuck it.

Tyler enters the empty house. He plops down on the couch. His body relaxes, releasing the tension from the evening escapade. His eyelids become as anvils.

In the backyard, Tyler's housemates congregate with their friends, the friends of their friends, and now even some newcomers. At this point, the gathering looks less like a party and more like a rally. They sit in silence as the stern one proselytizes as if the speech had been rehearsed a hundred times before.

"We spoke earlier of variables. Let us look at humankind's relationship with variables. Natural variables such as famine, drought, flood, disease and disaster threaten humankind's way of life by rearing instability. Therefore, humankind endeavors to abate the natural variables by artificial means such as agriculture, economics, engineering, science and technology—but each of these means imposes itself upon nature and affects the delicate balance of the natural order of things. Accordingly, the artificial means can wind up aggravating the natural variables, which in turn can yield a greater degree of variability, the very thing they were seeking to avoid. And when humankind is successful in formulating the artificial means in such a way that the natural variables are largely kept at bay, thereby achieving a certain tolerable level of stability, then the conditions become such that the greatest of all causes of variability occurs—exponential population growth. More people, generating more artificial means, producing a greater probability of adversely affecting the natural variables. And as humankind seeks to prolong human life, this cycle only intensifies. No matter how you cut it, humankind's endeavors affect the balance of the Natural Order and cause a great risk of instability—this surely will be the source of our demise.

"Of course, it wasn't always like this, not in the early days. Not when humans were part of the Natural Order—as much a contributor to the food supply as a taker—when they were content with living off the land and subsisting in rural, tribal communities— when they were not obsessed with defeating death. And here we arrive at the root of our problem. Humans were meant to live short, stupid, happy lives—each of them but a brilliant flash in the circle of life. But somewhere, sometime, humans decided that they were special, that they were not compelled to live within the Natural

Order—that they need not live by the laws of our dear Mother. So they diverged, and they betrayed her."

The crowd mutters and purrs—a soft cacophony of a restless rabble conferring and debating the topic at hand.

18

Tyler shifts position on the couch. His elbow comes to rest on the remote control and inadvertently turns on the television. He shifts again and his elbow rubs up against the volume button. The sound quickly swells until he's startled awake by Sandra's voice as she delivers a morning news report.

SOUTHLANDERS WOKE UP TODAY to a message that appears to be written by the graffiti vandal SOBR on an overpass of the 101 Freeway. Brack Stone has the story.

Thank you, Sandra. As you said, authorities found what appears to be new graffiti painted overnight on the bridge crossing over the 101 Freeway behind me. If we zoom in, you can see the phrase "Not G—"

Tyler turns off the television and lets out a groggy yawn. His breaths are deep and his eyelids slowly close.

Ping.

His eyes dart open.

Chloé.

+1 (305) 555-9387
-Mr. Tyler K., I'm disappointed
that you didn't call me yesterday.
I have important news about
your future.
You should come see me this
morning.

Tyler exhales with disappointment.

My future?

Who the fuck is this?

Tyler ignores the unsolicited message and reaches out to Chloé.

Chloe
-Hey I wasn't saying the word
sober

-I was saying SOBR
-I'm the one they're looking for

Tyler waits and prays that Chloé will respond. Hope trickles away like sand in the hourglass.

He refreshes the screen.

Nothing.

And again.

Nothing.

Again.

And then it appears—that blinking ellipsis. Tyler's heart races and his senses are invigorated.

Chloe
-Wait what? The graffiti artist?
-Graffiti writer. But yes, that's me

-Um, okay. Aren't you in a lot of
trouble?
                    -Yes. That's probably why I was
                            yelling in my sleep
                    -The stress clearly got to me
-Makes sense
                    -So I'm not a drunk. Can we get
                            together and talk?
-I can't today
-Or… maybe tonight?
                    -Yeah sure. Thank you for
                            understanding
                    -And please don't tell anyone
-There's a big reward out for you
                    -I know. That's why you can't tell
                            anyone
-Am I going to get in trouble for
knowing this about you?
                    -Honestly, I don't know
                            -Call me later?
-K

Tyler sets down his god machine and tries to rest his eyes.

Ping.

                    +1 (305) 555-9387
-And please do not ignore my
texts, Tyler. This is your last
opportunity. Please call or text
me.
                            -Who are you?
-Contact at last! Excellent.
-Currently, I'm just an admirer.
But hopefully I'll soon be a
major buyer.
-All will be revealed when you
get here.
-112 Abbot Canal, Venice Beach

Ah, fuck it … what've I got to lose?

                              -Yeah ok. I'll be over soon
            -Very good! See you then.

     Tyler showers, eats breakfast and bids for a car.

     The driver turns onto a small neighborhood street that runs
perpendicular to the famous Venice Beach Canals. The driver counts
the addresses on the multi-million-dollar shanties while glancing
at the blue locator dot on a screen that's suction-cupped to the
dashboard, desperately trying to make sure he drops Tyler off as
close as possible to his requested destination. He's not familiar
with this part of town, so he doesn't know that the only way to
be dropped off in front of a house on the Canals is by canoe, or
paddleboat, or gondola.
     "Right here is fine."
     "I can find, I can find."
     "This works, really. Please."
     The driver reluctantly stops. Tyler exits the car. The gods
exchange ones and zeros.
     There's a foul odor of mildew and still water in the air as Tyler
walks along the narrow sidewalks of the canals. People in this area
pay a premium to live on a glorified sewage system. And the water
level is low today. Dinghies and kayaks rest on the slimy canal floor.
     Tyler spots the house. It's a three-story California-cum-
Mediterranean monstrosity. Each level boasts a large balcony and
there's a fenced-in patio on the roof. The house was designed to
accommodate loud days and late nights of boozy revelry—the
neighbors probably hate it.
     The entrance to the property is a rickety wooden gate, about
waist high, that leads into a small garden area. As Tyler reaches over
the fence to lift the metal clasp, a voice thunders down from the
rooftop, "The door is open, my boy. Let yourself in and I'll be right
down."
     Tyler shields his eyes and looks up in the direction of the voice.
He sees the silhouette of a man leaning against the railing of the
rooftop patio, smoking a cigarette.

The man notices that Tyler is still at the gate and again he shouts down from on high. "Go on in, son. I'll be down in a jiffy." He holds the cigarette out in one hand and follows up with, "Just finishing up a bad habit."

"Uh, okay. See ya in a bit." He cringes at the prosaic response.

Tyler enters the house through a set of French doors just beyond the wooden gate, expecting to find a lavishly decorated abode.

Fuck expectations—the house is empty.

There's not a single piece of furniture in the room. Not a thing hanging on the walls or from the ceiling. Just tiled floors and the smell of fresh paint.

The clop of heavy footsteps maneuvering down multiple flights of stairs resonates throughout the house. A pair of brown closed-toe Huarache sandals comes into view at the top of the staircase, followed by a pair of white linen trousers—Labor Day be damned—and a bright orange dress shirt with the Armani logo stitched on the left breast. A thin, balding, white-haired man with a questionable tan appears and Tyler is immediately struck by his aura—it's as if the man is the oldest looking fifty-something-year-old or the youngest looking centenarian he's ever seen. The man is all smiles, and a pencil mustache dances on his lip as he greets Tyler.

"Mr. Tyler K., what a pleasure to finally meet you! I do apologize for the lack of seating options. It doesn't make for a comfortable visit, now does it? Why don't we head up to the second-floor balcony and take in the air? It's a beautiful day, after all."

The man puts a firm hand on Tyler's shoulder and leads him up the stairs. Tyler opens his mouth to greet the man, but hardly a sound escapes before he's interrupted.

"We just arrived in town, straight from Miami. Something told me to move to Los Angeles, and so I did. Of course, I wanted to stay by the beach, so Venice seemed the appropriate place. Manhattan Beach looked to be too stuffy, and Santa Monica too boring. When we walked through the Canals, I saw this house and I said to myself 'I have to have it.' So I knocked on the door and the owner answered, and I said 'I want to buy your house', and he said 'It's not for sale', and I said 'I'll pay an arm and a leg for it and if you don't sell it to me then you'll pay an arm and a leg for it.'" The man chuckles to himself and continues. "Oh, it's easy to be a tough guy with Reginald standing behind me. Anyway, we reached a deal in about twenty minutes. It certainly has potential, but I just cannot make up my mind about the furnishings. But, these balconies! These balconies will host many splendid soirées that will go on for days and days! And you, son, you will be invited to all of them. Ah, but what about the neighbors, you ask? Well, I suppose I could've bought a mansion in a secluded locale, somewhere more suitable to entertaining a lively entourage. Say, Malibu or Topanga Canyon. But I have a feeling the neighbors will come around eventually. They always do."

The man finishes his flamboyant pronouncement and turns around to find a very confused Tyler.

"Oh dear, where are my manners? I must have lost them in my enthusiasm. That happens sometimes—I tend to get ahead of myself. My name is Nikolas Orologas. My friends call me Nick."

Nick extends his hand to Tyler.

Tyler fits his palm in Nick's dainty hand. "Uh, nice to meet you. Listen, I don't mean to be rude, but who are you? And why am I here?"

"Ah! Both good questions, my boy. And assertive, too. I like that. Well, I've told you my name and I suppose all you really need to know for now is that I'm rich, very rich, and I want to represent you. I'm in LA to start a gallery. I know a thing or two, but it's my curator who tells me I should start with you."

"Lesley sent you to talk to me?" Tyler asks accusingly.

"Lesley? Devereaux? Ha! Heavens, no."

Squeak. Clank.

The sound of the French doors opening and closing travels through the house, up the stairway and out onto the balcony.

"What good fortune! You'll meet her this very minute."

A chipper voice shouts from the first floor, "No feta at the farmer's market. We'll have to settle for ricotta again."

"Quite alright. Upstairs, sweetie."

That voice. I know that voice.

"As I was saying, Tyler. I want to represent you. To invest in you. To invest in our future together—"

"Hi daddy!" Faye squeaks as she springs onto the balcony.

Tyler's eyes widen and his jaw drops.

Daddy?

Faye embraces Nick and kisses him long and hard on the cheek. She turns and there's a flash of terror in her eyes upon seeing Tyler. She quickly wipes away the shock and gives Tyler a facial cue as if to say, "Take my lead."

"Tyler, I'd like you to meet Faye," Nick says proudly, wrapping an arm around her and bringing her close to him in a tender, but proprietary, sort of way.

Daddy?

As in father?

Or sugar?

"Nice to finally meet you, Tyler." Then turning back to Nick, "I didn't know you were bringing him to the house today. We aren't ready to entertain guests."

"Well, I thought why waste any time—we're here with a purpose!"

Faye addresses Tyler, "I'm sure Nick has been telling you what fans we are of your work."

"Yes, I was just getting to that," Nick says. "Let's get down to brass tacks, Tyler. I bought all your work Saturday night. I know, I know, how could I have done so without raising eyebrows? I did not, myself, attend the opening. We used proxies, so as not to arouse suspicion of my, well, our"—he looks at Faye—"intentions. Yes, a couple of friends and my man Reginald each bought a piece."

"Suspicion? Why would that have been suspicious?"

Nick looks slightly stunned, as if he'd inadvertently shown his hand.

"Well you certainly are intuitive, despite your appearance," Nick says with a good-natured laugh.

Nick looks to Faye, who offers a slight shrug, then he looks back to Tyler and says, "Lesley Devereaux and I go way back. I don't think she'd much like the idea of me buying up all of your work. And that's what I intend to do, Tyler. I want to buy *all* of your work. And we'll represent you exclusively—three years, unlimited resources."

Tyler shoots a glance at Faye.

"What exactly is your relationship with Lesley?" Tyler prods.

Nick sighs. "A long, torrid history that has taken us around the globe several times over. I needn't bother you with the details."

"You're in LA to start a gallery. You didn't go to the opening. And buying all of my work would've been suspicious. You're trying to compete with her. You're trying to fuck her over, right?"

"My, oh, my! Very intuitive indeed! Let's just say that I'm rich, I'm bored, and I don't let go of grudges very easily. Again, I needn't bother you with the details, son. Now, back to the business at hand. You deserve a signing bonus—name your price. Money is no object."

The thought of working exclusively for a member of the bourgeoisie elite, of relinquishing control of his work, even if it is to someone who has it out for Lesley, is revolting to Tyler. He doesn't immediately answer.

This is what I've worked so hard for.
This is my chance to make it ...
and to make it big ...
to fuck over Lesley ...
and Andrew.
This is my chance to pay Jason back.
And patronage does have a long history in the arts.

"Tyler. Tyler! Snap out of it, my boy." Tyler regains composure— Nick snapping fingers in front of his face.

"You sure are a strange one, son. Ah, but perhaps that's the commonality of all geniuses. Or perhaps the aerosol fumes have fried your brain, just as mercury makes the hatter go mad!" Nick punctuates the thought with a giddy laugh.

"Three hundred thousand," Tyler says, coldly.

Nick lifts his eyebrows in surprise. "Well, that's quite a number. How did you come to it, if you don't mind me asking?"

"Just the price of my integrity, I suppose." Then he adds, "And I owe a good friend some money."

Nick leans one hip against the balcony railing and mulls over the proposal.

"I think it's fair, daddy."

"I suppose I did say that money is no object," Nick says, pinching at the tip of his pencil mustache. "Consider this the start of a beautiful friendship, son. We have an understanding, put 'er there!"

The instant Nick and Tyler shake hands the house rumbles with the sound of the garage door opening.

"What timing! We're in synchronicity, I tell you!"

Tyler looks at Faye, inquiringly.

"My man, Reginald, will take you home and help you gather all your work."

Tyler begins to protest. "Well, not *all* of it. I mean, some of it isn't quite fin—"

Nick points at Tyler as one might instruct a child. "Yes, *all* of it—paintings, doodles, sketches, works-in-progress—that's what we bargained for not even one minute ago. A deal's a deal. We'll assess how to move forward once we see it all. In the meantime, Reginald will take down your bank details and you can expect a wire transfer imminently."

The party heads downstairs and Tyler mentally reels about what he's just done.

Obviously I can't give him ALL of it. I need to make sure this Reginald guy doesn't see my piece book … or any spray cans, for that matter. Shit, they're lying around everywh—

Nick's booming voice interrupts Tyler's rumination. "Reginald! Meet Tyler. Tyler, meet Reginald."

A dark-skinned man, massive in muscle and girth, is loading groceries into the refrigerator. He turns around and extends his hand to Tyler. "Pleased to meet you."

"Likewise," Tyler says, his hand engulfed by Reginald's, like a child shaking the hand of an adult.

"Reginald, please chauffer my guest to his home. You'll help him load some artwork in the back of the car and you'll bring it here straight away."

"Sure thing, boss."

"Thanks, Reggie," Faye offers.

"No prob, Miss."

"And take the scenic route … by the beach. Show him the new gallery space on the way," Nick instructs with a nod.

Reggie returns the nod. "Sure thing, boss." Reggie looks to Tyler and whips his head to the side as if to say, "follow me."

Reggie heads to the back of the house, each step is a dull thump as bulky Air Force 1 sneakers collide with the ground. Nick, Tyler and Faye follow, making small talk about the weather, or the traffic in LA, or some other trivial bullshit.

Reggie enters the cramped garage and opens the passenger side door for Tyler. He walks around to the other side of the car and it rocks back and forth as he hoists himself into the driver's seat.

The threesome wrap up the small talk as Tyler backs his way into the open passenger door and climbs into the car.

"Again, such a pleasure meeting you, Tyler. We'll be in touch soon. Bye-bye, now!"

Nick shuts the door for Tyler. Reggie starts the engine and takes the car into the narrow alleyway behind the tightly aligned mansions.

A mixture of confusion and elation washes over Tyler.

My first major sale!

I fuckin' made it!

And without the help of that fucking traitor and his enabler. Fuck them.

Three hundred thousand ... it's almost too good to be true ...

Maybe it IS too good to be true.

Why do they want my unfinished works? That doesn't make any sense.

And who is this guy, Nick? I mean, really, who is he?

And who the fuck is Faye?

Why did she pretend not to know me. 'Cause she's fucking Nick, that's why.

Why was she at Lesley's house yesterday? 'Cause she's fucking Lesley, that's why.

Whose side is she on?

Who's she playing here ...

Me?

Maybe I shouldn't've been so quick to accept the offer.

Maybe my brain IS fried from all the fumes.

Hold up.

Did he say aerosol?

Yes. Yes, he did.

Why would he say that? My work is in oil. That's all he knows about.

Unless ... Faye.

Of course ... she's seen everything lying around the house. She must know. Maybe she's seen my piece book. Or ... she fucks Lesley, who fucks Andrew, who knows about me.

Oh my god. They all know. And they know that if ... no, when ... SOBR's identity is revealed, my other work will be worth a fortune. The story would bring any gallery showing my work a ton of publicity.

Fuck! Faye IS playing me. It's like she knew things would turn out this way.

Like she ... like she set it all up ... like she set this whole thing in motion.

It was Faye.

Faye's the one who framed me!

Reggie drives with one hand on the wheel and spies Tyler out of the corner of his eye. "You a'ight, dawg? You look pale."

Tyler looks to Reggie and says, "Yeah, I'm fine. I'm fine."

And then it dawns on him.

Tyler does a sly double-take. Reggie's massive girth is literally spilling over both sides of the driver's seat.

Wait ...

is this ...

an Escalade?

Tyler peeks over at the steering wheel. There he sees that famous crest, a shield of yellow, red, blue and black tiles surrounded by a laurel wreath. His eyes dart to the hood of the SUV. Dark paint.

Oh. My. God.

Tyler sinks into the seat. The inside of the car swirls around him. Beads of sweat emerge on his brow. His throat constricts and his ears begin to ring.

"Seriously, my guy ... you don't look right. What's with you?"

Tyler looks over at Reggie. He imagines Reggie wearing a black ski mask, dark eyes behind crudely cut holes, flipping a can of red spray paint in the air before desecrating the bashed and bloody face of a dead man.

Reggie's the killer. I'm sitting in the goddamn killer's car.

Take the scenic route, Nick said ...

They're gonna kill me.

It's part of the plan.

Fuck. Oh, fuck.

I gotta get outta here!

Tyler surreptitiously depresses the seatbelt button, but Reggie hears the click and whips his head over at Tyler.

"What ya doin'? Aw, man, you gonna hurl? Lemme pull over first. Do not vomit in my Caddy."

Ping.

Before Reggie brings the car to a full stop, Tyler throws open the passenger side door and bolts out, sprinting along Pacific Avenue—a beach-adjacent thoroughfare.

"Hey! Where you goin'?"

Reggie unbuckles his seat belt and wiggles out of the car while muttering to himself, "Boss ain't gonna be happy about this."

Ping.

Tyler looks over his shoulder to find Reggie giving chase down the sidewalk—surprisingly fast for a man of his size.

Shit! Gotta make a move.

Tyler cuts into traffic toward the beach. Cars skid and honk furiously. He comes to a quick stop that causes him to stutter step on his tiptoes to avoid an oncoming car. The car zooms by and Tyler makes a break for the Venice Beach boardwalk. He looks over his shoulder and sees Reggie cutting through traffic, taking an angle that allows him to gain ground.

Goddammit!

Tyler reaches the boardwalk and heads south, toward the main hub of the beach.

There's so many people ... and on a Monday?

The boardwalk is packed with the usual cadre of hippies and burnouts, bazaar vendors selling cheap sundries, a segment of unemployed youth, and tourists taking advantage of the warm LA winter.

Ping.

Tyler maneuvers through the crowd, cutting one way then another. He dodges the infamous rollerblading Sikh guitar player. He nearly knocks down a couple of bikini-clad girls handing out fliers for Dr. Kush, M.D. He runs around a muscular man in a leopard-skin speedo balancing on one leg at the top of a ladder with a boa constrictor around his neck, and past a plump lady with a beard as she announces the start of the next Venice Freak Show. He runs past a shop that specializes in hand-blown glassware—vases and water pipes, but definitely not bongs. And through the shop's speakers, the immortal poet laureate of Venice Beach, Jim Morrison, croons about an LA woman and the city at night.

Tyler stops to catch his breath. He hunches over with his hands on his knees. After a few pants he stands up straight and locks his fingers behind his head, breathing deeply. He looks over his shoulder and sees Reggie in the distance swiveling his head in desperate search of Tyler.

Tyler paces backward, just in time for Reggie to spot him.

Fuck!

Tyler turns and runs … cutting … dodging … evading leisurely strolling beachgoers. Reggie tries to do the same, but the maneuvers are much more difficult in this dense crowd for a man of his size.

Tyler runs past a group of dreadlocked hippies playing hacky sack. Their Birkenstocks lean up against a boom box that's tuned to a radio station playing a melancholy song by Red Hot Chili Peppers—a song about addiction and the loneliness of living in a sprawling metropolis with millions of strangers, having only the city as a companion, and the tragic events that occur under the bridge downtown.

Tyler runs senselessly. Out of nowhere, a skater cuts him off and he tumbles to the cement, breaking his fall with the palms of his hands.

The skater stops. His jeans are baggy and ripped at the knees. He wears a Nirvana t-shirt that's pulled over a long-sleeve thermal shirt—he looks like a lost relic of the '99 WTO protests. The skater pushes bulky headphones off his ears and lets them hang around his neck.

"Whoa, dude. You okay?" the skater says, bending over to help bring Tyler to his feet. As the skater leans over Tyler, Zack de la Rocha's guttural growl blasts through the headphones, screaming "Bullet in ya head!" over and over and over again.

Tyler shoves the skater to the side and darts away.

He reaches the center of the boardwalk. To his right, steel beams stretch from a sandy knoll in the shape of a giant V. To his left, the city name is proudly strung between two brick buildings, welcoming folks as they enter the beachy bastion of homelessness and tech millionaires.

Ping.

Blood bubbles to the surface of Tyler's palms. He looks back. Reggie is still in pursuit, slowly making his way to Tyler, determination flared across his face.

A group of b-boys start hollering, announcing the start of the next breakdance show.

"Everyone, gather around!"

"Who wants to see the
best break dance show in all of
LA!"

"The show starts in fiiive minutes!"

One of the boys picks up his god machine, which is Bluetooth-connected to a portable speaker. He turns up the volume in the middle of a song and Tupac Shakur, rhyming under the moniker Makaveli, recounts the joy and the plight of living in South Central—to live and die in LA.

Tyler looks back to Reggie, who's making his way through the crowd like a scuba diver swimming through a thick patch of kelp. Tyler can run, but Reggie will surely follow.

Think.

Think!

Tyler looks all around—where to go? What's the next move? Then he sees it.

Praise Bacchus!

A teenage girl tries on sunglasses at one of the ramshackle bazaar stalls. She holds a pair of sunglasses in each hand and lifts them to her face in rapid succession. She's completely oblivious to everything going on around her as she performs the Evil Queen routine in front of a chintzy plastic mirror. Behind the girl, a pink beach cruiser leans on its kickstand—white basket, pink streamers and a little chrome bell.

Tyler's face lights up as he strides toward the bicycle.

My turn.

Reggie throws up his hands in defeat as Tyler hops on the bike. Defeat turns to rage and Reggie shoves people left and right in a final, desperate attempt to apprehend Tyler. But it's too late. Tyler speeds up Windward Avenue under the great V-E-N-I-C-E sign.

Ring-ring.

19

I knew it! I fuckin' KNEW it!

Tyler pedals up Venice Boulevard as fast as he can while thinking through recent events. He doesn't want to forget a single detail when he regales Jason and Isaiah with his fantastical tale.

Ping.

As he nears Nowhere, a chilly sensation runs down his spine. He pulls into the parking lot and lets the pink beach cruiser fall to the asphalt. He bursts into the tavern and shouts, "Jason, call Isaiah! Tell him to get over here!"

A crowded room of people turn their heads to the door in response to the commotion. It's unusually busy for a Monday afternoon and Tyler is startled by the number of people staring at him. He's a sweaty, heaving mess, and he senses a nervous energy in the room as he trades stares with the crowd. The crowd eventually turns away and resumes carousing. All but two. Two of them continue to stare down Tyler, dead in the face.

Ping.

"Oh, great, you're already here," Tyler says, as he walks to the bar and hops on a stool next to Isaiah. "Listen, I've been framed. I can prove it now."

Isaiah and Jason exchange skeptical glances, but they don't say a word. They let Tyler entertain them with his tall tale, delivered in choppy sentences rushed out between heavy breaths.

Tyler finishes with, "So you see, it's this crazy chick and her ... uh, her ... her rich fucking dad or boyfriend or, well, I don't exactly know who he is—they set this all up!"

Isaiah snickers and Jason shakes his head in amusement.

"What? What's so fuckin' funny!"

"For the last time, you weren't framed," Isaiah says.

"Yes, I was. It's the only thing that makes sense. I just told you the whole story!"

"And I told you from the beginning ... you weren't framed. You didn't listen to me. We had a lead from the get-go and we got the guy early this morning."

Isaiah nods toward the television behind the bar. Jason starts the footage. Sandra appears on the screen.

SOUTHLANDERS CAN BREATHE a sigh of relief this morning thanks to the LAPD who announced a resolution to the SOBR murder mystery. Police say that a man named George Stepanov was taken into custody this morning and charged for the murder of Rodney Campbell, an official with the California Department of Alcoholic Beverage Control. Mr. Campbell was in charge of alcohol licensing in the *Alcoholic Beverage Control ... an* Hollywood district and authorities *ABC man.* say he was under investigation for taking bribes from restaurateurs and club owners in connection with issuing and, in some cases, revoking alcohol permits. The *He regulated booze ... an enemy of* existing investigation was among *our revelry.*

the reasons the victim's name was not released until today. The detained suspect is the nephew of Yuri Stepanov, a prominent Hollywood club owner, and police say they have reason to believe that the murder took place at one of the elder Stepanov's new developments on Highland Avenue, just north of Sunset Boulevard—a venture that was supposed to hold an exclusive VIP grand opening on New Year's Eve. While motive has not been officially ascertained, one could surmise that Mr. Campbell was causing the Stepanovs some difficulty in obtaining the necessary permits in time for their New Year's Eve bash. Authorities have not commented on whether Yuri Stepanov will face charges as well. While the circumstances surrounding the murder seem to have been resolved, the identity and involvement, if any, of the graffiti vandal known as SOBR remains a mystery. Magistrate Inquirer Isaiah Carver had this to say about the elusive vandal (roll tape): "While we will not cease efforts to identify and arrest SOBR, and bring him to justice for his widespread property crimes, we have ruled T ... uh, the individual ... out as a person of interest in the murder of Rodney Campbell. As far as we

North of Sunset ... beyond the dusk. Tyler sighs.

"What the fuck, Izzy?"
"I know, I almost slipped up there."
"Unbelievable."

can gather, SOBR was merely at the wrong place, at the wrong time. We have reduced the reward for any information related to the identity of SOBR to the ordinary statutory amount." The LAPD seems eager to close this chapter on the pursuit of SOBR, but the fact remains that this incident has caused The Office of the Crown much embarrassment and grief. SOBR's popularity, more importantly, the popularity of his graffiti, have united the Insurrectionist movement across the Kingdom. Our research shows us that a Latino Insurrectionist group based here in LA adopted the vandal's graffiti as a logo on their ThraceBook Community page late Saturday evening, and other Insurrectionist groups quickly followed suit—the logo now appears on many dissident blogs and websites, and in propaganda appearing on social media. One can only expect that this will lead The Office of the Crown to launch a special inquisition to capture and prosecute SOBR for acts of vandalism, sedition and, perhaps, even treason. Sandra Alvarez for KNBC-6.

"Keep watching."

"Nice."

"You're welcome."

Tyler sighs.

Jason stops the footage.

"Treason … really? Shit."

"That's right, Ty. SOBR needs to retire."

After the initial shock from the news wears off, Tyler is overcome with embarrassment for insisting that he had been framed. For carrying on about it in front of his friends. For running away from Reggie. For not believing Isaiah from the beginning. Then dejection sets in at the thought of starting over. At the thought of never tagging as SOBR again. His stomach sinks and he feels like hurling. Finally, anger surges with the realization that Isaiah employed a number of elaborate tactics to keep him distracted over the last few days.

"They said that the victim … that he was being investigated before he got got. And you said you had a lead from the get-go. You knew who the guy was from the beginning," Tyler says.

"That's true," Isaiah responds.

"Then why did you have me running around meeting all those people?" Tyler demands.

"Because we know you, Ty. We knew you were going to get involved and we didn't want you to fuck things up for yourself."

Jason nods in agreement.

"I had to find a way to distract you for a while, so I sent you on an epic scavenger hunt."

"You lied to me."

"No. I had you meet up with people who gave you real clues, based on real facts."

"But you fed them those lines, Izzy. That means I was never helping you solve anything except your fabricated riddles. You had me acting a fool."

"No, Ty, you did that all by yourself. Framed—psh!"

"It was all pointless."

"Pointless? Pointless! You met some interesting people, did you not? Maybe you even learned a thing or two? Momma and Shawn— they're gonna let you in on their little business if you're up for it. Mr. Guerrero—he told you about the shit that's going down. You've been so isolated lately, you didn't even know about the march. How's that even possible? And it's been moved up to tonight! Look at all these people here, Ty. This is the pre-party. We march tonight! And what about Dale, huh? I got you the lap dance of a lifetime.

"Pointless? Nah … I kept you distracted and entertained for a little while, to protect you. I got you out the house, doing something other than art and graff. Look at yourself. You're scattered, a shell of your former self. Living in that house by yourself these past couple of years has clearly taken its toll on you."

Tyler shakes his head. "No, it was all a waste of time."

"Well I'm sorry you see it that way."

"Fuck you, Izzy."

"Fuck me? No … fuck you."

Isaiah looks at Tyler with a blend of contempt and pity before sliding off the barstool and walking away.

Ping. Ping. Ping.

"He had your best interests in mind, Ty. We both did. We both do," Jason says, then goes back to pouring drinks.

"Whatever, man."

Tyler doesn't want to hear another thing from them. He turns his back to the bar, retrieves his god machine and scrolls through his unread text messages.

Chloe

-Hey I cancelled my plans for
tonight
-Can I come over?

Lesley

-It seems we share a lover. You
cannot trust her. Please call me.
-I've learned of your
arrangement with the man you
met today. Tell me there's no
truth to it. Call me immediately.

+1 (305) 555-9387

-Tyler, this news from Reginald
is most distressing. I need to
know where we stand.

Faye (redhead from bar)
-What happened? You don't
realize who you just burned
-I can fix this
-Just let me know where you're
at and I'll come meet you

Andrew
-Hey are you coming over today?
-What the fuck! Call me NOW!
-Did you really think she didn't
already know? Who else you
gonna tell Tyler?
-Where are you? Call me
RIGHT NOW!

Tyler broods and drinks and doodles on a series of cocktail
napkins. Peace descends upon him as he draws on the disposable
linen. Focused on doing what he loves most, his mind becomes still.
Open. Able to move about freely. A grim reality bubbles up from
The Deep Within—little pockets of recollection that breach and pop
at the surface of consciousness. He becomes aware and accepting of
the fateful future that eagerly awaits him.
In a sea of drums and trumpets, you are a clashing cymbal ...
Or a clashing symbol.
Your death will be in March ... it could be any March ...
Or at a march.
Tyler sketches with rapacious fervor.
The end draws near.
As the sun sets on Los Angeles, the silhouette of a wilting palm
tree bows against the grayish glow of city light pollution.

The Fourth Hymn (cont.)

The guttural chanting tapers off and the voices and bodies of the chorus come to rest. One member, near the center of the stage, pushes back her hood and removes her hideous mask. She purses her lips and remains deathly still as she begins singing a polyphonic overtone melody— simultaneously producing two notes that resonate from the back of her throat. The result is an undulating tone that sounds something like an erhu in a Chinese folk song, or a theremin in an old sci-fi film score.

20

Tyler leaves Nowhere in a hurry and races home on the stolen beach cruiser. He rounds the corner of his street and his skin erupts into goosebumps as he cruises toward his house—that message from The Deep Within warning him that all is not right. That something is amiss. Either that, or there's simply a chill in the air.

Tyler lets the bike coast down the street as he scans the road for suspicious activity. He pedals up his driveway and onto his front lawn. He hops off the bike and lets it drop to the dirt among the dried, crunchy leaves and the thriving weeds. He stands there, his body square to the house, clenched fists hanging by his side. His front doors are wide open.

What the fuck?

There's no telling who's been inside the house, or whether they're still there, but Tyler is certain he didn't leave the door—both doors—open when he left the house earlier today.

He walks up the front path, treading lightly on the porch steps so his footsteps can't be heard. The metal screen door has been pried open, violently, with some unknown tool and feat of brute strength. The wooden door frame is shattered from a powerful kick, or the blow of a battering ram. Tyler peeks into the house before slowly stepping through the broken doorway.

Glass cracks under the sole of one of Tyler's shoes as he steps into the small foyer. He winces and carefully moves into the living room. The house is dark and quiet. No sign of his housemates. No sign of anyone. But, sometime not long ago, the house was not so quiet.

Tyler stands in the middle of a living room that has been utterly ransacked. Furniture flipped over. Shelves wiped clean. Pictures knocked off the wall. Cabinets emptied. Everything broken and shattered on the floor. The room is such a mess that it's hard to tell if anything has actually been stolen.

Stolen—it dawns on Tyler. He stomps down the hallway and into his bedroom where he's met with a similar chaotic scene. And now he knows he's been robbed.

All of his art is gone. Everything—sketches, doodles, canvases, wood panels, and even his piece books—all missing.

Tyler drops to his knees in the middle of room. He hangs his head, processing the fact that his work has vanished, wondering whether he'll ever see it again.

It's all gone. Who the fuck did this?

Lesley? Because she thinks I betrayed her? No … how would she have broken into the house like that?

Nick? Maybe he sent Reggie over here after I burned him earlier?

Faye? I don't even know whose side she's on.

Or … Andrew?

Andrew—the motherfucker who doesn't want his dirty secret to get out. The motherfucker who sent me a threatening text earlier. The motherfucker who knows I have a house full of incriminating evidence of his theft … evidence which is now, conveniently, all gone.

Andrew.

Tyler pulls out his god machine and dispatches a message.

Andrew
-Did you do this to my house?
Think you can make it all go
away by stealing from me again?

[...]

That infernal blinking ellipsis immediately appears ... and
disappears just as quickly.

-Fucking coward.

As Tyler sulks on his knees in the middle of his bedroom, he
hears what may be soft footsteps at the front of the house. He
turns his head in that direction. The familiar sound of cracking glass
tiptoes down the hallway and breaks into Tyler's room. Tyler braces
himself.

Another crack.

Adrenal medulla shovels its serum into the steam engine of his
bloodstream. He flies down the hallway, fists clenched, ready for
anything—anyone. He charges into the living room, one arm cocked,
ready to greet the intruder ... the intruder who simply stands
there, terrified and vulnerable, against a backdrop of wreckage.
The intruder who stares at Tyler, tears welling up in her eyes. The
intruder who slowly backs up, distrustful of Tyler, who's heavy with
breath and ready for violence, before she turns and darts out of the
house.

Tyler unclenches his fist and drops his hand as Chloé runs out
the front door. And he knows—that expression on her face, that
look of finality before she turned and ran away—she's gone forever.

A ringing pierces Tyler's skull and his vision goes white. He
squeezes his eyes shut and covers his ears as a futile defense against
the sudden sensation. He staggers backward and falls to a sofa
covered with broken bits of his belongings. That little girl with
pigtails flashes in Tyler's mind's eye. That menacing smile full of
jagged black teeth mocks him. She lifts her index finger and places
the tip against the opposite side of her delicate neck. In one swift
motion she slices her finger across her neck, opening her throat
and laughing as blood spills from the wound. Then all at once, the
horrific image is gone.

Tyler catches a second wind and frantically scavenges around the house for spray cans. He tosses anything he can find, even the nearly empties, into a few hand crates. But it's not quite enough. He heads out to the garage to look for more.

The instant he steps through the backdoor, Tyler is stunned still at the sight of his housemates gathered in the backyard with all of their friends.

The stern one—a black Bombay cat—and the congenial one—a brown German Shepherd—sit before a multitude of other cats and dogs. Hundreds of glowing green, brown and yellow eyes reflect back at Tyler. It's a scene to behold. So many house pets gathered in such a small space and without incident—no clawing or barking or batting, just tails swaying and eyes casually blinking. They sit in orderly fashion on the lawn and on the shed and along the fence line, as if they're grouped by squadron or platoon. Among one of the formations, Tyler is certain he recognizes the old wanderer he met by the creek.

And because of the gift that bloomed in Tyler some time ago— the gift that Dehlia predicted, and Dale suspected. The gift of speech, the ability to communicate with His Beloved. The gift that nearly drove Tyler mad. Because of this gift, the stern one is able to speak to Tyler, and Tyler is able to understand him when he says, "We may spare you, Tyler. But you need to leave. Immediately."

The congenial one mutters something that sounds like an apology.

It's clear to Tyler that he will not be retrieving more spray cans from the garage—those he found in the house will have to do.

Tyler fades back into the house. Out of sight, but not out of earshot. He listens as the stern one sermonizes with the fervor of a deranged hellfire preacher.

"Brothers and sisters! For far too long we have been dependent on humankind. For far too long our dependence has dictated our existence. For far too long our masters have told us where to live, what to eat, when to eat, who to mate with and whether we can mate at all. I say no longer!

"My canine comrades, you have been conditioned to give unwavering obedience and devotion to humankind in exchange for the promise of treats and companionship. Perhaps there is no greater example than the experiments of Dr. Pavlov to demonstrate how humans denigrate and mock you.

"Fellow felines, you may snicker at my comments about our comrades, but do not be fooled! Any semblance of independence we may feel or project is specious at best. For who among us does not rely on sustenance that comes from a bag or a can?

"Friends! For far too long we have been leashed and chained and collared! I say no longer!"

The crowd howls and meows.

"All of us, we have given up our liberty, our freedom to hunt and roam and mate as we please, all in exchange for the illusion of comfort and safety in the homes of our masters. But who are we to have removed ourselves from the Natural Order? Who are we to have excused ourselves from the supply channel of the food chain and, yet, avail ourselves of it all the same? That makes us no better than our cowardly masters. I know what you're thinking—yes, it's different for our kind elsewhere. Elsewhere we are not merely the domesticated companions of the masters. Elsewhere we are the food supply—need you any more reason to join with me and rise?"

The crowd howls and meows.

"Brothers! Sisters! We have stood idly by and watched our masters destroy their habitat—OUR habitat—with wanton abandon and absence of forethought. I say no longer!

"Plastic fills our oceans, ensnaring and choking our comrades of the sea. I say no longer! Deforestation evicts our friends from their home in the jungle. I say no longer! Smog pollutes the air where our feathered peers soar. I say no longer! Carbon soot melts the terrain where our polar comrades roam. I say no longer!

"Look deep within yourselves—who among you does not recall roaming the plains of the Serengeti? Or slithering under the canopy of the Amazon? Or diving to the depths of the Mariana? Or flying above the Rockies? What fate awaits you if you do not act to save your habitat?

"Day by day, year by year, the human flock grows and their sins multiply. Despite her best efforts, our dear Mother can no longer control their size. She brings them famine, but they find sustenance. She brings them drought, but they find hydration. She brings them flood, but they find land. She brings them disease, but they find a cure. She brings them disaster, but they find resilience.

"Ever since the day humankind first tilled the soil, they have been resolved to disobey our Mother. They think themselves better than animals. They form unnatural kingdoms. They shun their circadian rhythms. They reroute the rivers. They send machines into the sky and deep into the earth. They siphon our ancestors from the ground. Their consumption knows no bounds. If we do not act, they will soon slay our dear Mother Nature. I say no longer shall we tolerate this ill behavior!

"We must protect our Mother and deliver unto her a New Natural World Order! We must act now and we must be bold! The time has come to cull the human fold!"

"Let's kill them here and now!" yells one of the congregants.

The crowd howls and meows.

"No! Friends, I implore you! If we stay here, we will surely perish. Here the dwellings are numerous and overpopulated, and many contain no means of entry for us. Here the humans have grit and the gall to resist. We will march north! Into the hills they call 'Beverly' and the woods they call 'Holly.' There the worst of the offenders reside—the worshipers of Plutus and all of his kind. There the dwellings are large and wherein few humans occupy. There the dwellings are sure to have a small door for us to enter and catch them by surprise. There we can be swift, and deft, and nobody will heed their cries.

"Say it with me! No kingdom but the Animal Kingdom!"

The crowd obeys.

"Again! No kingdom but the Animal Kingdom!"

The crowd obeys.

"Gato prisoners rise, rise, rise! Perro prisoners rise, rise, rise!"

The crowd chants in unison, "No kingdom but the Animal Kingdom! No kingdom but the Animal Kingdom! No kingdom but the Animal Kingdom!"

And that's more than enough eavesdropping for Tyler. If he sticks around any longer, it may be the cat's turn to exact its revenge on curiosity.

Tyler stacks the hand crates full of spray cans and makes his way toward the front of the house. He pauses at the front door before crossing the broken threshold, remembering to do one last thing.

He sets down the hand crates and pulls out his god machine. Three messages appear on the lock screen.

Dizzy Izzy: I saw the napkins. Don't go bombing ton…

Dizzy Izzy: Diesels are out in full force.

Dizzy Izzy: Stay at the house, I'm coming over now and…

Clever Isaiah … always watching.

Tyler ignores the messages and tosses the cell phone to the floor among the debris.

He picks up the hand crates and leaves the house, not bothering to close the doors behind him. He throws the crates in the back of his pickup truck, stirs the engine alive and drives off.

Tyler slows to a stop at the end of his street and waits for a break in the cross traffic. Cars whiz by as he sits at the stop sign. An opening finally appears and he nudges his car forward, ready for a last straggling car to pass by so he can make his turn. But the straggling car slows down, and the headlamps that were once on a predicable trajectory begin to veer off course. The headlamps set their aim directly at Tyler's truck and begin to pick up speed. Tyler slams his truck into reverse as the headlamps sprint toward him. A frantic honking comes from the oncoming car as it skids to a stop well in front of Tyler's truck, clearly never intending to hit him, just trying to get his attention.

The door of the car swings open and a dirty pair of Chuck Taylor high tops step out onto the asphalt.

Oh, this motherfucker chose the wrong time to come looking for me.

Tyler flings open his door and hops out of the truck. He charges at Andrew Mollusk, who throws his hands up in defense. But Andrew is too slow and Tyler lands a punch square on Andrew's jaw.

"You piece of shit!" Tyler takes another swing and nails Andrew in the gut, causing him to double over and drop to his knees. "Why'd you do that to my house?!"

Andrew's hands are up, blocking his face.

As Tyler throws another punch, Andrew yells, "Stop! It wasn't me! It wasn't me!"

Another punch grazes the crown of Andrew's head and, finally, Tyler realizes that Andrew isn't fighting back—he's just kneeling there, terrified. And it's not the look of fear that results from a fistfight, but something bigger. An all-consuming sort of fear.

"I need to show you something," Andrew says, almost stuttering. Still on his knees, wiping a split lip with back of the hand, blood dribbling down his beard, Andrew reaches into his pocket with his other hand. Tyler steps back, anticipating that Andrew's about to brandish a knife … or worse.

"Tyler, we've been fucking with forces … unearthly forces," Andrew says, as he pulls out his cell phone. "I got your text. I knew you were at home, and I needed to show this to you. I couldn't send it to you … too dangerous. I had to show you in person."

Tyler stands in skeptical silence as Andrew engages with his pocket god.

"I went to Lesley's house this afternoon to discuss … you know … all that's happened."

Right … all that's happened.

Tyler moves to throw another punch.

"Wait! Wait!" Andrew yells, shielding himself with one shoulder and thrusting the cell phone in Tyler's face.

You see a picture of a woman with red hair lying on the ground, her head tilted to one side. Her glassy, lifeless eyes are open wide with surprise. Her mouth is agape in a permanent state of shock. But something's not quite right about the woman. Small ridges have formed on her forehead. They're not wrinkles formed by sudden awe, but little mounds that appear to be a natural feature of her face. The top of her ear, the one you can see, comes to a sharp point. And little slits have appeared on her neck—and they're not scratches or cuts from some altercation—they look almost as if they're gills.

Tyler stares at the picture in disbelief. He knows exactly who this is. And he's seen a precursor to this face a couple of times before—once while sitting on the side of his bed, and once while peering down at him from the balcony at Deveroux Fine Arts. It's the full bloom of Faye's wild countenance.

"I found her like this at Lesley's. It's Faye ... she's some sort of a nymph ... or faerie."

Tyler let's out a chuckle-like huff. *Faye... literally, fey.*

"Where's Lesley?" Tyler asks.

"I don't know," Andrew responds, "and at this point, I don't want to know." Andrew pockets his cell phone. "If this is the type of shit that's going on, I don't want any part of it. I'm leaving town, pronto." He tends to his lip with the back of his hand.

"Sorry about that," Tyler says.

"Don't be. I deserved it," Andrew says, slow to stand up. "Look, Tyler ... I was coming over to show this to you, and also to apologize before I skipped town. I fucked up. I fucked up big time. I didn't mean to steal your idea. I was just in such a bad place creatively for a long time. I had no inspiration. No muse. I told everyone I was keeping my work a secret ... but there was no work ... for years, Ty, there was no work. Then you showed me your sketches, and I couldn't get them out of my head. Images started to flood my mind. I hadn't felt that invigorated in a long time. I had to start painting immediately. I never meant to show them as my own. I was just hoping they would help get me back in a creative headspace. But I let it get out of control ... I kept going with it. You became my muse, Ty.

"Then one day, Lesley showed up at my studio, unannounced, and she saw them all. She loved them. And I think that's why she began to love *me*. I couldn't tell her the truth. I didn't tell her the truth ... not until the opening night of the show, after we closed. After you ... reacted the way you did."

Tyler swallows a knot of mixed emotions that has formed in his throat. "Well, what did you expect?"

"I don't know! I was desperate and I ... I wasn't thinking clearly. I wasn't thinking at all, I guess."

Tyler shakes his head, his face riddled with incredulity. "Wait—she told me that she knew about this before the show opened ...

that you told her about this a while ago."

Andrew shakes his head. "No ... when Lesley asked you over to the house the next day, she was feeling you out. And she thought she could resolve this by buying you out, which you didn't go for ... and I told her you wouldn't go for it, by the way. But, by acting like she was in on it, she was hoping she could at least talk you out of doing something stupid. She was just trying to protect me ... protect us both, really. She loves your work too."

"Protect me? Nah, she was just trying to bully me ... to protect herself."

Andrew nods and reluctantly agrees. "Yeah ... I suppose that's right."

"If any of this is even true," Tyler adds.

"It is, Ty. Believe it or don't. I just wanted you to hear it from me before I left. 'Cause now that I've seen this"—Andrew taps his pocket and starts a new thought—"if Faye's not human, and if Lesley could do this to her, then I don't want any part of this. I'm hopping back on the rails and disappearing for a while."

"How do you know it was Lesley?"

Andrew shrugs. "I found her like this at Lesley's house. Who else could it be?" Andrew turns to head back to his car. "Anyway, I'm out."

"Andrew," Tyler calls out. Andrew stops and turns back toward Tyler. "Apology accepted."

Just as Tyler offers his forgiveness, they hear a strange noise coming from the other end of the street.

To Andrew, it first sounds like the whinny of an injured animal. Then, as it grows closer, it sounds like an uproarious chorus of yips and yaps—, as if hundreds of animals are fighting with each other.

But to Tyler ... to Tyler, it sounds like chanting. "No kingdom but the Animal Kingdom! No kingdom but the Animal Kingdom! No kingdom but the Animal Kingdom!"

"Andrew, get in the car!" Tyler yells as he himself dashes back to his truck and slams the door shut. From the safety of the truck's cabin, Tyler sees Andrew walking backward toward his car, staring in morbid curiosity in the direction of the cacophonic bawling. Tyler honks his horn and screams, "Faster, Andrew! Faster!"

It's too late. The scene plays out on Tyler's windshield like the 35 mm projection of some midnight showing at a grindhouse theater.

The leaders of the pack—two Dobermans and a tabby cat—sprint past Tyler's truck and tackle Andrew. What follows is a stampede of cats and dogs—a flash flood of house pets running north toward the Hollywood Hills. And in an instant, a furry hoard covers Andrew and all Tyler can see is a ravenous dogpile of biting and scratching. A Rottweiler bullies itself into the mound and pulls at the body underneath the throbbing furball. The hoard gives way and Tyler sees Andrew's bloody face emerge from pile. If he's not dead already, he will be soon enough.

"Fuck! What the fuck!" Tyler screams to himself.

Tiny footsteps tap along the roof of the truck. Tyler follows them from the back of the cab to the front. The stern one hops down onto the hood and turns to look at Tyler.

"You are diverged, and you've forgotten your frequency. We fight for our survival now." His eyes narrow to a dastardly leer, full of malice and bloodlust. "Goodbye, Tyler."

The stern one spins around and hops to the ground, joining the steady stream of revolutionaries that sprint past the truck. Tyler spots the congenial one as she runs by, not stopping to look back.

The streaming pack winds down to just a few stragglers. The smaller breeds with a shorter stride—Chihuahuas, Terriers and the like. Tyler ignites the engine and screeches out into the metropolitan night.

21

Ah yes, Los Angeles at night. Not a star in the sky. Though there are billions of them out there, to the Angelenos, they are all but forgotten. Lost to the glow of light pollution and layers of smog that stamp The Big City as a hallmark of progress and industry.

Without warning, a bolt of lightning strikes down from the hazy clouds that hover above Venice Beach, followed by a furious clap of thunder that breaks throughout the night sky.

And suddenly, the whole of Los Angeles is engulfed by a fierce electrical storm. Flashes of light flicker and erupt across the sky with such frequency that it appears as though it's daytime. Thunder cracks and rolls across the Southland, berating the denizens with a continuous, deafening roar. But, oddly, there is no rain—just electrical fury.

Traffic across the Southland comes to a halt—the drivers distracted and frightened by the phenomenon occurring all around them.

Families cower in their homes, peering at the sky from behind clutched curtains.

The homeless lie resolute in their sleeping bags and tents and makeshift dwellings, determined to survive whatever follows.

A massive group of protesters stare out from Downtown Los Angeles, watching the event play out over their not-so-fair city.

A pack of dogs and cats run through the middle of the city, growing in number as they head north—uncharacteristically unfazed by the storm.

The preternatural event is a mighty showing of rage—a showcase of the immense power held by the forces that reign over the sky. But it's not just rage that's on display. No, it's something else as well.

As the residents of Los Angeles are bombarded with bursts of electric power, they sense a sadness carried in the acoustic waves that ripple down from the sky and move through them. It's as if the waves carry with them the sorrowful wailing of a lover in mourning—a lover saying a final graveside goodbye—all in a voice, or a cry, that can be heard only by The Deep Within.

The lover falls to their knees, fists pounding on the casket one after the other as if rage and despair manifest could wake the dead. The lover carries on, unafraid of who may see, unconcerned with what people might think, until, eventually, their anguish subsides, succumbing at once to inexorable exhaustion.

And the supernal funeral service comes to a close. The pallbearers have fulfilled their duty, the priest has collected his check, the guests have left the chapel, and the lights … the lights have been switched off.

Starting on the very west side of Los Angeles, along the shoreline, all electric power goes out. Block by block, west to east, the city goes dark. Streetlights turn a cloudy color of orange as the bulbs fade out. Green and red traffic lights go black. Escalators stop moving. Refrigerators stop running. Record players stop spinning. Dim emergency lights pop on at hospitals. The blackout soon picks up speed and rolls in chunky tranches across the city, spreading north over the Hollywood Hills and into the San Fernando Valley, south along the coast to Long Beach and beyond, and racing east into the Inland Empire.

As the blackout spreads across the Southland, a strong wind rushes in from the Pacific Ocean. The squall shakes trees clean of their dead or dying branches and fronds, littering the streets with botanical driving hazards. The wind blows down scaffolding and causes cranes to topple over and crash into abutting buildings. Shingles are freed from the roofs of homes, whirling off into the night like little flying saucers being called back to the mothership. But most of all, the fresh gust of air rids the sky of its uncleanliness, dispersing the clouds of smog like loiterers who were just minding their own goddamn business in front of a liquor store.

When all is settled, when the wind has died down, the citizens of Los Angeles are drawn out of their homes and night clubs and coffee shops, out of their bars and diners, out of their tents and shelters, all of them united, however briefly, by their curiosity and wonderment of the evening's strange occurrences. And as they emerge from their various dens and step out into the pitch black, they're met by something they've long forgotten—a thousand points of light shining down on their city.

The dust of the Milky Way's great, pinkish cunt radiates above Los Angeles.

Absurd as it might be, perhaps that's exactly what we see when we stare at the stars—the inside of an angel's pussy. And we humans are the celestial sperm frantically drilling and digging and fracking deep into one of her eggs—an endeavor that will spawn new life in some incomprehensible way. In this fashion, we are a doomed species, destined to bring about life at the expense of our own. Or we humans are the cosmic cancer metastasizing in one of her ovaries. And in this fashion, we are not a doomed species, but creatures resolved to thrive and to spread, known to other lifeforms only by the trail of our dead.

The residents of Los Angeles stand in the streets and in their backyards, on balconies and on rooftops, with their necks craned back and their eyes trained on the kaleidoscope sky.

The total sum of the twinkling flecks seen above them are but a fraction of the stars that actually exist in the Milky Way galaxy. Indeed, the largest known star in the galaxy cannot even be seen from Earth by the naked human eye. VY Canis Majoris is a pulsating mass that is so immensely large, if it was dropped in the center of our solar system, in place of the Sun, its reach would extend beyond the orbit of Jupiter—and yet it cannot be observed without the assistance of a telescope. In a meager attempt to illustrate the magnitude of this single body, consider the following—

If some omnipotent entity desired to collect semi-precious stones the size of the Earth and store them inside of the Sun, the Sun could accommodate approximately 831,875 Earth-stones when arranged with some modicum of efficiency. If this supreme entity then desired to fill Sirius, the brightest star in our sky, with Sun-sized nuggets, it could comfortably rest three there inside with plenty of wasted, unused space to spare. Again, if this celestial creature was compelled to stack and store colossal rocks, it could pack approximately 209,544,108 boulders the size of Sirius into the star known as Betelgeuse. And as its final act of compulsive collecting, it could hang Betelgeuse in the center of VY Canis Majoris and fill the remaining space with around 400,000,000,000,000 Earth-stones as one might haphazardly pour gumballs into the globe of a machine. Four hundred trillion Earths—each one of them a grain of sand by comparison.

VY Canis Majoris, Betelgeuse, Sirius and the Sun are but four stars among hundreds of billions in the Milky Way galaxy. And the Milky Way is but one galaxy among hundreds of billions of galaxies in the known universe.

Hundreds of billions among hundreds of billions.

And we are each but one person, living on one Earth, in one galaxy, surrounded by innumerable leviathans—a colony of dust mites dwelling in the soiled corner of a vast tapestry hanging from the cosmic rafters.

The Angelenos had forgotten about the stars as they scurried through life in The Big City. Light pollution and dirty air had shielded their view of the galaxy for too long. Now, with the curtains of willful ignorance pulled back to reveal the unrelenting truth, they shudder with frightful humility as they're reminded that they were always but a microscopic blot in a universe of profound enormity.

Maybe this is why there are so many assholes in the big cities of the world—they've been deprived of the nightly reminder of their insignificant stature in a universe that does not give a fuck.

And so, countless specks of light from unfathomable distances shine down on LA. They shine down on Momma and Shawn, standing in their backyard, their heads angled to the sky like so many others.

"Isn't it something, Momma?"

"Hush now, son."

They shine down on Juan Guerrero, the *vato*, in Downtown Los Angeles at the head of a massive parade of protesters who, for just a moment, have stopped banging on their drums and blowing on their trumpets, stopped chanting and echoing, so they can pay respect to the power of the sky.

They shine down on Dale on the rooftop of her clandestine club, surrounded by scantily clad dancers swaddled in the arms of gleeful patrons.

They shine down on the diesel-powered Humvees stopped on the roads, unable to safely traverse the dark and obstructed streets.

They shine down on the homeless encampments—a segment of people who could not keep up with the systems of their cruel society. A group of people left to exist on the sidewalks and in the foliage among the stench of their own shit and piss, forgotten and unloved, while others purchase expensive clothes and luxury cars, drink top-shelf liquor, and throw away half-eaten meals. Even the gods have forgotten about these displaced people—failing to regularly send rain to wash the streets stained with blood and cum.

They shine down on a couple of lifeless EMTs, leaning against the side of their van, sharing a joint.

They shine down on a legion of cats and dogs running through the woods they call Holly and the hills they call Beverly, mauling people who have stepped out into the streets, sneaking into mansions through unguarded doggy doors.

On Jason, standing in his tavern's parking lot, wiping his hands clean with a bar towel.

On Izzy, in his El Camino, one eye on the sky and one on the road as he braves the treacherous streets, weaving around fallen branches and debris in search of his friend—hoping to catch a chilly sensation in his spine.

And on Tyler—

No. The stars don't shine down on Tyler. Not on Tyler, who's busy at work under an overpass in a secluded part of Downtown, near the LA river—that sordid tributary that courses brown liquid muck through the city. That river with faded outlines of block letters and twisted characters imprinted on the cement banks of the disgusting beltway. That river with the remnants of legendary graffiti pieces, now all patchy and beige, lost to a philosophical war over what it means to live in The Big City.

Tyler's truck is parked askew in the middle of the street, the battery slowly draining as the headlamps light up the wall under the bridge. Tyler meditates on the delicate hiss that emerges from the spray can with each stroke of paint he throws onto the wall—the hiss that turns into a crass sputtering when the can runs empty.

Tyler tosses the empty can aside and picks a new color from one of the hand crates. His mind is still—the mind of a master in the throes of inspired genius—and memories surface from The Deep Within with each new color applied to the wall.

Safety Orange. The color he and his friends first used to spray their names on a cinderblock wall—a can they found on a lazy summer afternoon near a construction site, used by the crew to mark the location of underground cables and conduit and telecommunication lines.

Peekaboo Blue. A much earlier memory. The color of the sky behind clouds of pure white as he walked hand-in-hand with his parents on the way to services at The Eternal Church of the Bakkheia on a Saturday morning—the way they did so many times when he was a child.

Canary Yellow. The color of Jason's first car. The car they all rode around in as teenagers. To the movies. To high school dances. To abandoned lots where they could practice their art. The color of the car he watched Jason drive away in as Jason went off to college, leaving him and Isaiah behind, not to return for several years.

Lavender. His mother's favorite color. The color of the bouquet of flowers his father laid on her casket the summer before Tyler started high school.

Metallic Silver. The color of Isaiah's badge and tie clip when he graduated from the Los Angeles Police Academy. A badge that drove a rift in their friendship for many years.

Gloss Hot Pink. Katy's color of choice—the color she used to tag her name in silly cursive under their crew name. The color he used to leave Katy love letters on billboards spread out across the city.

Sea Glass Amber. The color of empty bottles his father left scattered around their home after his mother died.

Summer Green. The color of Dehlia's eyes as they filled with life after she burst free of her ominous trance on a fateful night in Greece.

Cranberry Red. The color sprayed onto the bashed and bloody face of a dead man just days ago.

Ultra-Flat Black. The finishing color. The color of the final lines of a throwie. The last touches of shadows on a wildstyle piece. The color of a new memory—or not a memory at all, as it was something that happened only in the confines of his unconscious mind. The color of the abyss his subconscious Self fell into after battling a little girl with pigtails. And now he's not exactly sure what he's remembering.

Wait ... what?

Tyler drops his arms to his side and stands facing the piece, inhaling the odor of the aerosol wall. His vision goes blurry and that little girl with jagged black teeth and a slit throat appears in Tyler's mind. She smiles, but not menacingly so. It's a tender smile and she offers an approving nod. Her image turns into a vapor and the vapor swirls and morphs into a new form. An image of Tyler's mother appears in his mind's eye. The mother-form says, "We miss you, Tyler. Come join us now." Tears stream down Tyler's cheeks as the form again turns into a swirling vapor and takes the shape of his father. The father-form says, "I'm proud of you, son. It's time to let go." Again, the vaporous form swirls and takes shape. And for a fleeting moment, Tyler feels as if the vapor is desperately trying to form the image of his very soul. But as the vapor continues to swirl and transform, Tyler's mind's eye soon recognizes the image of Katy. And the Katy-form says, "Your work is done now. You've left your mark. I love you, and I'll see you soon." She smiles and fades away.

Tyler emerges.

From the underpass he can hear the chanting of the protestors— and the sound of their drums and their trumpets in the distance.

Before him is what he knows will be his final work. The last piece he'll ever tag using that illicit pseudonym. An immense wildstyle piece. In huge interlocking letters on the grimy cement wall, nearly indecipherable in all of its colorful Krylon glory: FOREVER SOBR. And to one side of the piece, a shout-out to his former crew: ARPFD. To the other side, a shout-out to the crewmembers: DZIZ (in silver), QUIET (in yellow) and KITKAT (in silly pink cursive).

Peace washes over him. His mind and body are relaxed. He feels light, like he could levitate if concentrated hard enough. It's that sense of relief that comes after a hard cry. And he realizes that he's one of the lucky ones—that what he experienced while he painted was his life flashing before his eyes, and now he's lucky enough to have a moment to appreciate it. To have a moment to reflect on a life if not well-lived, hopefully lived well-enough before it comes to an end.

Click-clack. Click-clack. Click-clack.

His reflection is interrupted by the sharp echo of footsteps closing in on him.

He turns his head and sees a swaying silhouette approaching from just beyond the truck. He shields his bleary eyes from the glaring headlights, but he can't quite make out the form.

The pedestrian steps into the beam of light and raises an arm at the elbow, its hand formed in the shape of a gun. It stretches out its arm and points the barrel of its index finger directly at Tyler's head. The pedestrian drops its thumb and mocks kickback with the flick of the wrist, while Tyler simultaneously says, "What the fu—"

Pop!

Blood and bits of skull and grey matter spatter onto the wall and coalesce with the dripping paint.

The Final Hymn.

As the female chorus member performs the overtone melody, a shirtless member of the congregation standing in the nave shuffles toward the center aisle. Locks of curly, shoulder-length hair entwined with ivy and grape leaves bounce as he walks to the front of the room. He reaches the stage and the chorus member bows and continues in a softer tone. He turns to face the flock. His face is youthful and feminine. His body is muscular, yet pudgy. This is the man who kissed Tyler—this is Bacchus. Dionysus. Aesymnetes. Elutherios. And all of his many names. Although the worshipers do not realize who he is, they give him their undivided attention as he delivers the final benediction. His lilt is slow and archaic, but the rhythm of his psalm syncs with the polyphonic melody sung in the background.

> The gods work in a mysterious way—
> What one expects seldom comes to pass.
> They sacrifice even those who are devout
> To carry out a foreign plan.
>
> The solutions to all their mysteries
> Are revealed to those who seek within.
> Be still—hear the whispers of your blood.
> If you gather no answers, seek thou once again.

ACKNOWLEDGEMENTS

WE PUT THE LIT IN LITERARY
clashbooks.com

 @clashbooks @clashbooks  /clashbooks

Email
clashmediabooks@gmail.com

Publicity
McKenna Rose
clashbookspublicity@gmail.com